U0093851

哈福

哈福

哈福

哈福

老師沒有教，考試一定考

英文慣用語

〈多益、GEPT、高中、學測
托福、IELTS、統測必備〉

附QR 碼線上音檔
行動學習 即刷即聽

喬納森 ◎著

哈福

老師沒有教，考試一定會考的慣用語

英語句子，越短越好，1、2 個字慣用語，超好用；老師不會教，考試一定會考。本書網羅沒有「文法邏輯」的常考慣用語，讓您英文高人一等，考遍天下無敵手。

* 說英語，越短越好

你學英語很久了嗎？會不會在跟外國人溝通時，還是覺得有障礙、有距離呢？普遍英語教科書教你的內容雖然正確無誤，但是有時仍難免流於刻板、公式化。希望把一種語言真正學好，除了必備的字彙、文法、句型外，你更需要花功夫了解當地的一些通俗用語，雖然有些用語並不正統，或者你在字典裡根本找不到，但是很多字彙早已深入當地文化，廣為流行，通用。學會外語的慣用語，能夠幫助你的外語更生活化、更實用，不論是自我進修或者對外聯繫，都能有絕對加分的作用 。

* 什麼是慣用語

情用語是指光看字面，無法立刻判斷意思的片語。常常兩個再熟悉不過的單字，組合在一起，意思就完全不一樣了。這些片語中，動詞片語又佔大多數。一般人常常猜不透到底這些片語的真正意思為何？比方說：all thumbs，這兩個單字一般人都認識，不過它的真正意思，你猜到了嗎，答案是：「笨手笨腳 」。

的確令人匪夷所思，沒有一些想像力，還真猜不出正確的意思。不過這也就是英語趣味的地方，需要傷點腦筋，但弄懂了之後，要忘記也不太容易。慣用語是英語非常重要的組成要素，要學到英語的精髓，能不能流暢運用慣用語，是重要關鍵之一。本書收錄了近一百五十個，由二個字組成的慣用語，讓讀者從簡短、基礎、實用的角度切入，迅速熟悉老美常用詞句，進而能流利運用。

* 關於本書

本書目的在幫助讀者，瞭解各種單字或雙字英語慣用語的意思，除了中英文慣用語定義解釋，每則慣用語皆附有例句和對話，可以幫助記憶，運用自如。內容編排方式以字母排序，更方便讀者查閱和使用。另外，為了使讀者學習最正確的發音、語調，本公司特地聘請專業美語教師，錄製精質全書朗讀線上MP3，發音標準、口齒清晰，同時練好聽力及口說能力，完全掌握英語慣用語及標準發音。

學好慣用語，才是英語實力的展現，聽說讀寫高分的關鍵，本書讓您徹底學會慣用語，現學現用，考試、自學、聊天，都都有加分作用，多益、GEPT、高中、學測、托福、IELTS 必備。

＊本書使用方法

✎ 單數與複數名詞

有一些慣用語可當成名詞使用。如同一般的名詞，這些通常有單數形及複數形。例如：

➲ 單數

He is a homebody.（他是個居家型的男人。）

She is an early bird.（她是個早起的人。）

➲ 複數

They are homebodies.（他們是居家的男人。）

We are early birds.（我們都是早起的人。）

✎ 動詞時態：

有些慣用語中含有動詞，這些動詞可能需要根據它們在句子中的用法而做變更。例如：

➲ 現在式

I hope it doesn't fall flat.（我希望它不要徹底失敗。）

ime flies when you are having fun.（快樂時光總是過別快。）

➲ 過去式

His idea fell flat.（他的主意徹底失敗了。

While we were working, time flew.（當我們工作時，時間飛逝。）

✎ 代號說明

[something]〔某物〕: 示其他的字或能用在此慣用語中。

[also :]〔也 :〕: 表示同一句慣用語的另外一種說法。

[opp :]〔反義 :〕: 表示具有一相反意義的對應慣用語。

〔非正式〕: 表示此慣用語用於非正式場合。

[n]〔負面 / 否定〕: 表示大部份以英語為母語的人認為此慣用語是負面或否定的。

✎ 描述

[c]〔常用〕: 表示慣用語的多種意義中最常用的那一種。

[v :]〔動詞 :〕: 表示此動詞通常與慣用語一併使用 ; 這些動詞並非慣用語本身的一部份。

[often neg.]〔通常為定〕: 表示雖然本慣用語有肯定用法，但通常以否定型態出現一例如 :「變胖」(carry weight) 常見的用法是「沒有變胖」(doesn't carry weight)。

使用慣用語一定要確定，自己完全理解其真正意思，否則萬一錯用，可能是雞同鴨講，各自表述，卻完全沒有達到溝通的目的。在適當時機套用慣用語，不但令你的英語詞彙更加生動，通常也會另對方大開眼界，對你擅於運用英語的能力印象深刻。

【附贈免費 MP3 線上音檔】

本書的外師標準錄音，以「免費 QR Code 線上 MP3 音檔」，全新呈現給讀者，行動學習，即掃即聽，隨時隨地，可提升聽說讀寫能力，英語實力進步神速！

編者謹識

目錄 Contents

MP3-2

* Achilles heel

弱點

中英文詳解

a weakness in someone or something that is usually considered perfect

完美的事物或人的唯一弱點

➲ He is an outstanding basketball player, but free throws are his Achilles heel.

他是一位傑出的籃球選手，但是罰球是他的致命傷。

➲ Though he is extremely brave, snakes are his Achilles heel.

他英勇無比，但是碰到蛇他就束手無策了。

實用會話

A Hey, Brian, how're you doing?
嗨，布萊恩，你好嗎？

B Great, Janet. How's your diet going?
很好呀，珍娜。妳的節食計劃進行得如何？

A It's going ok. But, I keep eating M&M's.
還不錯，但是我還是照吃 M&M's 巧克力。

B They always were your Achilles' heel.
你碰到 M&M's 就沒輒了。

A I know, and I can't seem to stop at just one handful.

我知道，而且我都要吃一大堆才過癮。

* acid test

嚴峻的、決定性的考驗

中英文詳解

a test whose results are without doubt

結果令人不容置疑的考驗

➲ The mayor says everyone approves of the job she's doing. The acid test will be whether she gets reelected.

市長說每個人對她的政績都表示肯定。是否果真如此，就看她能否連任了。

➲ John says he's learned from his mistake. The acid test will be whether or not he does it again.

約翰說他已經由錯誤中學到教訓。他能否經得起考驗，就看他是否會再犯了。

實用會話

A Sally, what's wrong?

莎莉，怎麼啦？

B I'm not sure I can handle this class. It's so hard.
我不確定我能不能唸好這門課，真的好難。

A You seem to do ok when the teacher asks you a question. You always know the answer.
可是老師問妳的時候妳答得很好，妳都知道答案。

B I know, but I have to study really hard every day. The mid-term exam will be the acid test of whether or not I have to drop the class.
我知道，但是我每天都要拼命唸書。等期中考考完，就知道我能不能過關了。

* all-nighter

通宵熬夜

staying up all night to do something, usually study
通宵熬夜做事，通常是指唸書（與動詞 “pull” 合用）

➲ I'm so tired because I had to pull an all-nighter last night.
我累壞了，昨天晚上我整晚開夜車。

➲ Getting the job finished will require an all-nighter.
這件工作要通宵才能趕完。

實用會話

A Sandy, why do you look so tired?
珊蒂，妳怎麼看起來那麼累？

B I had to pull an all-nighter to finish my research paper. It was due today.
我昨天熬夜趕研究報告，今天是交報告的日子。

A You've known about that paper for two months. Why did you wait till the last minute to do it?
妳不是兩個月前就知道要交報告了，怎麼拖到最後一分鐘才寫？

B I don't know. I always seem to wait till the last minute to do things.
不知道，我好像都是臨時抱佛腳。

* all thumbs

笨手笨腳的

中英文詳解

very clumsy, especially when using one's hands

笨拙的、手腳不靈活的，尤指需要用手操作的事

A

➲ I'm all thumbs today. I keep dropping my chopsticks.
我今天笨手笨腳的，筷子一直掉。

➲ When I get nervous, my hands start to shake and I become all thumbs.
我一緊張就會雙手顫抖，笨手笨腳的。

實用會話

A Will you please hurry and open the door? I have to go to the bathroom really badly.
快點開門好不好，我要上廁所，快憋不住了。

B I'm trying, but I can't get the key to go into the lock. Damn! Now I dropped the key.
我在努力了，可是我沒辦法把鑰匙插進鎖裡。不會吧！鑰匙掉下去了。

A Here, let me try it. You seem to be all thumbs today.
我來好了，你今天笨手笨腳的。

B I know. I don't know why.
是呀，我也不知道為什麼。

a

* anybody's guess

誰也說不準的事

中英文詳解

something no one can be sure about

沒有人能確定的事，大家都拿不準的事

➲ Whether the governor will win is **anybody's guess**.

沒人敢說州長是否會獲勝。

➲ It is **anybody's guess** whether we will be able to build the new school. It depends on the new budget.

沒人知道我們是否能蓋一間新學校，全看新預算了。

實用會話

A Dad, why aren't we moving?

爸爸，我們怎麼都不動？

B We are in a traffic jam. It doesn't look like we're going to be moving for a while.

我們碰到塞車，看起來我們好一陣子不能動。

A How long will we be stuck here? I'm bored.

我們會在這裡塞多久？我好無聊。

B I don't know, Scotty. It's anybody's guess. I'm not even sure why we have stopped.
史考特，我不知道，也沒有人知道，我甚至為什麼我們得停下來都搞不清楚。

MP3-3

* anything goes

有什麼不可以

中英文詳解

any kind of behavior is acceptable
任何行為都可以接受

➲ In the sport of ultimate fighting pretty much anything goes.
終極格鬥比賽幾乎容許任何攻擊動作。

➲ In today's world, it seems like anything goes when it comes to entertainment.
在今天這個世界，只要和娛樂扯上關係，似乎什麼都可接受。

實用會話

A These kids are driving me crazy. Why don't their parents stop them from running all over the place?
這些小孩快把我逼瘋了。為什麼那些做父母的不阻止他們亂跑？

B I don't know. When I was a child, my parents would never have let us behave like that.
我怎麼知道？小時候爸媽才不會讓我們這樣呢。

A Unfortunately, with many parents today, it seems that anything goes.
很不幸，對現在的父母來說，似乎什麼都可以。

B Yeah, anything except making your child behave!
是呀，除了管好自己的小孩之外，什麼都可以！

* as one

一致，與…成為一體

中英文詳解

a group behaving as if it were one person
一群人動作一致
（與動詞 act、move 或 speak 合用）

➲ When the teacher tripped and fell, the children all laughed as one.
看到老師跌倒，小朋友們一起哈哈大笑。

➲ The dancers moved across the stage as one.
舞者整齊劃一地在台上舞動。

實用會話

A Sam, what will help us win this election?
山姆，我們該如何贏得選戰？

B In my opinion, the most important thing is that everyone in the party speaks as one.
依我看來，黨內每個人要口徑一致。

B I'm not sure I understand.
我不太懂。

A In other words, what I tell the voters must be the same thing you're telling the voters. We need to be consistent.
也就是說，我和選民說的必須和你一樣；我們要一致。

* at half-mast

降半旗；（襪子上部或褲腿等）太短或掉一半

中英文詳解

halfway up or down (primarily used for flags, but can be used for other things as a joke)

上升或下降一半（主要指旗幟，也可做戲謔語）

➲ When President Kennedy was killed, all the flags were flown at half-mast.
甘迺迪遇刺後，全國降半旗。

➲ The boy ran out of the bathroom with his pants at half-mast.
小男孩褲子穿一半就衝出廁所，。

實用會話

A Did you hear about the governor?
你有沒有聽說州長的事？

B No, what about him? What happened?
沒有。他怎麼了？發生什麼事？

A He died last night. Apparently he had a heart attack.
他昨晚去世了，似乎是心臟病發作。

B Oh my! That's horrible. But, now I know why all the flags are being flown at half-mast.
天哪！真可怕！現在我知道了為什麼到處都降半旗。

A Yeah. They'll be that way until Friday.
是呀，到星期五之前都會降半旗。

* at loggerheads

爭吵

中英文詳解

in opposition to something or someone; in a confrontation with something or someone

反對某事或某人；與某事或某人對立

➲ Bob's parents were at loggerheads for years before they finally got a divorce.
巴伯的父母吵吵鬧鬧許多年，最後以離婚收場。

➲ Jane has been at loggerheads with her insurance company over fixing her car after the accident.
車禍後，珍和保險公司為了修車的事一直僵持不下。

實用會話

A How'd it go with your boss?
你和主管處得好嗎？

B Basically we are at loggerheads. She won't give me the support I need for the project. And, I told her I wouldn't do it until she does.
基本上我們很不合，她不支持我的提案；我告訴她，她不支持我就不做。

A Aren't you afraid she'll fire you?
妳不怕她開除你？

B No, because they need me. I'm the only one in the company who can do this job.
不會，他們需要我。公司裡只有我能做這份工作。

* back down

MP3-4

放棄，讓步

give up or surrender
放棄或投降

➲ Dora begged her father to let her go out with Simon. She finally had to back down and stop asking.
朵拉求父親讓她跟賽門出去。最後她只好放棄，不再懇求。

➲ Allen said he won't back down if his cousin tries to beat him up again.
艾倫說，如果表哥再打他，他不會讓步。

A Are you going to ask your boss for a raise again?
你還要向老闆要求加薪嗎？

B Yes. I really think I deserve it and I'm tired of him giving me excuses.
沒錯，我真的覺得那是我應得的，我不想聽他那堆藉口了。

A Well, you do deserve it. This time, don't back down if he says, "no."
嗯，你是該加薪了。如果這次他再說「不行」，千萬別讓步。

B I won't. In fact, if he won't give me the raise, I'll quit.
不會。事實上，他再不加薪，我就辭職。

* backseat driver [n]

說些無用建議的人，多管閒事的人

【負面】

a person who gives unwanted advice
說些無用建議的人

➲ Jeff has never changed a tire before, but he kept trying to tell me how to do it. What a backseat driver he is!
傑夫從來沒換過輪胎，還一直告訴我該怎麼做；他真是多管閒事！

➲ Stop being a backseat driver! I know what I'm doing.
不要多管閒事！我知道自己在做什麼。

實用會話

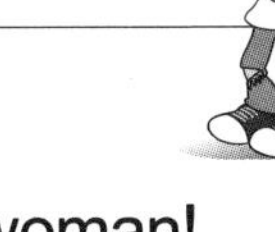

A Richard, be careful of that old woman!
理查，小心那位老太太！

B What old woman?
哪位老太太？

A The one going into that store over there.
那位走到那間店裡的老太太。

B Why do I have to watch out for her? She is going into a store on the other side of the street. I'm not even close to her. Stop being a backseat driver!
為什麼要小心她？她走進街那頭的店裡，又不是在我旁邊。不要再指揮我了！

* bird's-eye view

鳥瞰；概觀

中英文詳解

1. a view seen from high above something [c]
2. a brief overview of something

1. 從高處觀看事物【常用】
2. 某件事情簡要的觀點

B

➲ We got a bird's-eye view of San Francisco as the plane was landing.
飛機降落時，我們鳥瞰了舊金山的風光。

➲ The class only gives a bird's-eye view of the events of World War II.
這堂課只提到第二次世界大戰的種種事件概論。

實用會話

A This is my friend, Keith. He's visiting from the US.
這是我的朋友凱斯，他來自美國。

B Nice to meet you, Keith. How do you like Taipei?
你好，凱斯。你喜歡台北嗎？

C I like it a lot. We were just at the top floor of Taipei 101. It was cool! You can see the whole city.
很喜歡。我們剛去台北 101 頂樓，真酷！可以看到整個城市。

B Yeah, it is really nice. You get a great bird's-eye view of Taipei from up there.
真的很棒；你可以在那裡鳥瞰整個台北市。

b

* blank check

請某人全權處理，自由行動處理權

中英文詳解

the freedom or permission to act however one wishes

讓某人隨意行動的自由或特權。

➲ Irene hasn't been told how to run the office. She has just been given a blank check.

沒有人告訴愛琳該怎麼管理這間辦公室，她剛被授與全權。

➲ Being the president's son doesn't give you a blank check to be rude to people.

當總統的兒子，不代表你有權對人民粗暴無禮。

實用會話

A Karen, I need to speak to you.

凱倫，我要和你談談。

B What do you want, Dad?

你要談什麼，爸爸？

A Your mom and I are going away for the weekend. We are going to leave you in charge of your brother and sister. But, that doesn't give you a blank check to be mean to them.
我和你媽媽這個週末不在家，你要負責照顧弟妹，但是，那不代表你可以隨心所欲，對他們大吼大叫。

B Yeah, I know. You don't have to worry.
好，我知道，你不用擔心。

* born yesterday

沒有經驗的，笨的

中英文詳解

1. inexperienced; 2. stupid [c]
1. 沒有經驗的；2. 愚蠢的【常用】

⊃ I know how to drive. I wasn't born yesterday.
我知道怎麼開車，我可不是沒經驗。

⊃ Sometimes Pete acts like he was born yesterday.
有時候彼特表現得笨笨的。

實用會話

A Greg, you've had too much to drink and you are very drunk right now.
葛雷格，你喝太多了，現在醉醺醺的。

B So?
哦？

A Well, I think it would be best if you gave me the keys to your car. I'll drive you home. You shouldn't drive drunk.
你最好把車鑰匙給我，我載你回家；你不能酒後駕車。

B I know that! I wasn't born yesterday!
我知道！我不是笨蛋！

* buy (something)

同意，相信

中英文詳解

to believe someone or to accept something as true
相信某人，或相信某事為真

➲ She told me she didn't do it. But, I don't buy what she said. I think she's lying.
她告訴我那不是她做的，但是我不相信；我覺得她說謊。

➲ I'm having trouble buying the idea that the government is going to reduce taxes.
我相信政府會減稅，卻讓自己惹上麻煩。

實用會話

A Did you talk to Sue? Did she say why she wasn't at the party last night?
你和蘇談過嗎？她有沒有說為什麼昨晚沒來參加派對？

B Yeah, I saw her this morning. She claims that her car got a flat tire.
有，我今天早上看到她，她說他的汽車爆胎了。

A Hmm. Do you buy her story?
嗯，你相信她的話嗎？

B No way! She owns a motorbike, not a car.
當然不！她的車是機車，不是汽車。

MP3-5

C * carry weight (with someone)

（對某人）有影響力，具重要性

中英文詳解

to have influence with someone; to have importance for someone (often neg.)

對某人有影響力，對某人很重要（常是負面意義）

➲ Your idea is a good one. But, since you aren't a member of the management team, it will not carry weight.
你的主意不錯，但因為你不是管理團隊的一員，可能不會受到重視。

➲ Alex's opinion carries weight with me, since I respect him so much.
我非常尊敬愛力克斯，所以他的意見對我十分重要。

實用會話

A John just told me that the company was going to let 200 people go.
約翰剛剛告訴我，公司大概要裁員兩百人。

B I wouldn't worry about it. If John said it, it's probably not true.
我倒不擔心，如果是約翰說的，可能就不是真的。

A What do you mean?
什麼意思？

B John is known for making things up. So, what he says usually doesn't carry weight around here.
大家都知道約翰擅於無中生有，通常他說的話不足採信。

* cash in (on something)

賺錢，從…中獲利，利用

中英文詳解

to make a profit or earn a lot of money from something

藉某事獲利、大賺一筆

➲ Their stock is doing really well right now. If you are smart, you'll find a way to cash in on it.
現在他們的股票行情不錯，如果你夠聰明，就會知道怎麼大撈一筆。

➲ Unfortunately, it is too late to cash in on that clothing style. No one is wearing it anymore.
不幸的是，那種款式已經沒賺頭。現在沒有人穿那種衣服了。

實用會話

A Hey, Russell. What's up?
嗨，羅素，有啥新鮮事？

B Not much. I'm just working on a business plan.
沒什麼，我正在計畫要做一筆生意。

A Oh, yeah? For what?
喔，是嗎？是什麼？

B You know how juice bars are really popular right now? Well, I'm trying to find a way to cash in on that popularity.
你知道現在果汁吧非常流行嗎？我想投入這個市場賺上一筆。

A Just be careful that you aren't too late.
你要注意會不會為時已晚囉。

* catch cold

[also: catch a cold]

感冒

【也做：catch a cold】

中英文詳解

to get a cold (the illness)
得到感冒（這種疾病）

➲ I always catch a cold at this time of year.
每年這時候我總是會感冒。

➲ You should dry your hair before going out in cold weather. Otherwise, you might catch cold.
天氣冷的時候，出門前要吹乾頭髮，否則你會感冒。

實用會話

A Please turn off the air conditioner.
請關上冷氣。

B Why? It is hot in here.
為什麼？這裡這麼熱。

A I know, but I was just outside in the rain.
我知道，但是我剛淋雨回來。

B So?
所以？

A So... I'm soaking wet and I don't want to catch cold.
所以，我全身濕淋淋的，我可不想感冒。

* caught short

缺乏，不足，不敷需要

中英文詳解

to not have something that one needs at the moment, especially money
手邊缺乏急需之物，尤指金錢

➲ I was making a cake for my boyfriend's family, and I was caught short. I didn't have any eggs!
當時我正在做蛋糕給我男朋友的家人，卻發現東西不齊全，因為我一顆雞蛋也沒有！

➲ At dinner last night, Mike was caught short. He had to borrow money from Monica.
昨天晚餐時麥克忘了帶錢，只好向莫妮卡借錢。

實用會話

A Why are you so upset?
你為什麼這麼沮喪？

B I was on my way to Costco, when a cop pulled me over for speeding.
我開車去好事多，但是超速被警察攔下來。

A Oh, that is annoying!
喔，討厭！

B That's not the worst thing. I was caught short, since I forgot to bring my license with me. He gave me an extra ticket for driving without it.
那不是最慘的，我沒什麼前了還忘記帶駕照，他就再開一張無照駕駛的罰單給我。

* chicken out [i]

MP3-6

打退堂鼓

【非正式】

中英文詳解

to not do something because of fear (in this idiom chicken is used as a verb)

因為害怕而不做某事（“chicken” 在此做動詞）

➲ I was going to go skiing on my vacation, but I chickened out. I was afraid I'd break my leg.
本來想去滑雪渡假，我怕摔斷腿，就打退堂鼓了。

➲ When Teddy got up to make his speech, he chickened out and went running off the stage.
泰迪起身上台演講時臨陣脫逃，從台上溜走。

實用會話

A Did you ask Keith out on a date?
你有沒有約凱斯出來？

B Well, I called him. But, when he picked up the phone, I chickened out and hung up.
我打給他，但是他一拿起電話我就嚇得掛上了。

A Really? I can't believe it. You've wanted to go out with him for months.
真的？我不敢相信，你這幾個月一直想和他約會。

B I know… I know. I'm just afraid he'll say, "no."
我知道…我知道，可是我怕他會說「不」。

* child's play

極簡單、極易做的事

中英文詳解

something considered very easy
一般認為很簡單的事

➲ Last night's math homework was child's play. I had it done in 10 minutes.
昨天晚上的數學作業真是太簡單了，我十分鐘就做完。

➲ Getting my younger brother to lend me money is child's play.
跟我弟弟借錢簡直就是輕而易舉。

A Help! I can't get my computer to work. What is going on?
救命，我的電腦不會動，怎麼會這樣？

B Calm down, Jonathan, let me see it.... There you go! It is all fixed.
冷靜點，強納森，我來看看……好啦！修好了。

A How did you do that? I tried everything.
你怎麼弄的？我試了半天都沒用。

B It was child's play to fix. You forgot to plug it in, silly!
很簡單呀，你忘了插上插頭，笨蛋。

A Gee, I can be so stupid!
天哪，我怎麼那麼笨！

* cloak-and-dagger

陰謀的

involving secrets and secret planning
秘密的，有關陰謀的

➲ A lot of cloak-and-dagger stuff goes on in politics.
許多政治事件都有陰謀。

➲ The appointment of the new director involved a great deal of cloak-and-dagger activities.
新上任的董事牽扯到很多內幕。

實用會話

A Ok… I'm here. What do you want?
好…我來了，你要什麼？

B Did Jill see you leave the house? Does she know where you were going? She didn't follow you, did she?
吉兒有沒有看到你出門？她知不知道你要去哪裡？她沒有跟蹤你吧，有嗎？

A No, she doesn't know where I am. Now tell me, why all this cloak-and-dagger stuff?
沒有，她不知道我在那裡。你說，為什麼要這樣神秘兮兮的？

B Well, we are planning a surprise party for her birthday and we don't want her to know about it.
我們在幫她準備生日驚喜派對，不能讓她知道。

* cold comfort

敷衍的安慰

中英文詳解

no comfort or relief at all

沒有任何安慰或慰藉

C

➲ The plumber's promise that the sink is fixed is cold comfort. He has said that before and it keeps leaking.

水管工人保證水槽已經修好了，只是敷衍一下而已。他以前就說過同樣的話，可是還是一樣在漏水。

➲ I can pass the course, if I do well on the test. That is cold comfort, though, since I don't even understand the information.

如果考試能夠拿到高分，我這堂課就會及格。那這只是自我安慰罷了，因為我對考試的內容一點都不瞭解。

實用會話

A What's up, Brad? You look tired.

怎麼了，布萊德？你看起來很累。

B I've been up late recently trying to get my store finished. There is still so much to do before I open.

為了讓我的店能夠就緒，最近我已經連續熬夜了好幾個晚上。但是，在開幕前仍然有許多的工作要做。

A I'm sure you'll get it done. Besides, better late than never.

我相信你一定可以做好。況且，晚點開張總比永遠不開張好。

B No offense, but that is cold comfort. If I have to delay the opening, it will cost me a lot of money.
我沒有惡意，不過你說的話只是安慰我而已。如果要延開幕時間，我將會損失慘重。

MP3-7

* cold feet

臨陣退縮

中英文詳解

extreme nervousness or fear, usually preventing one from doing something [v: get]

因為非常緊張或害怕，使得某人無法去做某件事【動詞使用 get】

➲ I wanted to go bungee jumping, but I got cold feet.
我想玩高空彈跳，但是臨陣退縮了。

➲ Right before the wedding, James got cold feet.
就在婚禮前一刻，詹姆斯突然退縮了。

實用會話

A So, Frank, did you tell Emily's parents you wanted to marry her?
那麼，法蘭克，你向艾蜜莉的父母提親了嗎？

B Well, I took them to dinner at a nice restaurant. And, it was going really well. We were having a nice conversation...
嗯，我帶他們去一家高級餐廳用餐，而且一切都進行得很順利。我們談話很投機⋯⋯

A And?
然後呢？

B Well, her father asked me why I had invited them to dinner, and I got cold feet. I just couldn't tell them.
嗯，艾蜜莉的父親問起為什麼我要邀請他們吃晚餐，我卻臨陣退縮，說不出口。

* come out

[also: come out of the closet]

真相大白；出櫃

【也做：come out of the closet】

中英文詳解

1. to reveal one's secret;
2. to reveal one is a homosexual [c]

1. 將某人的秘密公諸於世
2. 公開某人是同性戀者【常用】

➲ Freddy came out that he is a big fan of ballet and opera.
弗瑞迪承認他超愛看芭蕾舞和歌劇。

➲ My best friend came out to me yesterday. I had no idea she was a lesbian.
我最好的朋友昨天出櫃了，我一點都不知道原來她是女同性戀。

實用會話

A Did you hear that Jack came out to his parents this past weekend?
你聽說了嗎？傑克在上個週末把他是同性戀的事告訴他父母了。

B No. I didn't know that. How did it go?
不，我沒聽說。結果呢？

A His parents were shocked he is gay. But, overall, it went better than he expected.
他父母聽到他是同性戀時，非常震驚。但是，整體而言，情況比他預期得好。

B That's good. Coming out to one's family is never easy.
那很好啊。向家人坦承自己是同性戀不是一件容易的事。

* copycat [n]

抄襲者

【負面】

中英文詳解

a person who imitates someone else

模仿他人的人

➲ Tony bought the same sneakers as Solomon. He is such a copycat.

湯尼買了一雙跟索羅門一模一樣的運動鞋。他真愛學別人。

➲ When we were younger, my cousin was such a copycat. She used to do everything my brother and I did.

我們小時候，我堂妹很喜歡模仿別人。她那時總是學我和我弟弟做一樣的事。

實用會話

A Wow, this is weird.

哇，真是怪了。

B What?

什麼啊？

A This robbery mentioned in the newspaper. It is almost exactly like the other five that happened last month.
就是報紙上報導的搶案啊。作案手法和上個月發生的另外五起搶案幾乎一模一樣耶。

B I thought they caught the robber that did those five.
我以為警方已經逮捕到犯下五起搶案的搶匪。

A They did. This must be a copycat thief.
沒錯。那麼這個搶匪一定是模仿之前的作案手法。

* cross swords (with someone)

（與某人…）爭辯

中英文詳解

to have an argument with someone
與某人發生爭論、發生口角

➲ I don't want to cross swords with you. Can we try to work this out calmly?
我不想和你爭辯。我們是不是可以試著冷靜地解決問題？

➲ George just crossed swords with the boss over the new employee benefits plan.
喬治剛剛針對新的員工福利計畫和他的老闆爭論。

實用會話

A Hey, what's up?
嘿，怎麼了？

B Oh, nothing. I just crossed swords with my mother again. It seems like it is happening more and more, lately.
喔，沒事啦。只是剛剛我又和我媽吵架了。最近，這種情形發生的次數好像越來越頻繁了。

A Uh, oh. What was it this time?
真糟。那這次是為了什麼呢？

B Oh, the same old thing. She thinks I should be married by now. And, I told her I would get married when I'm ready.
喔，還不是為了一樣的事。她認為我現在早該結婚了。可是，我告訴她，等我準備好我就會結婚。

* cry wolf [n]

發假警報

【負面】

中英文詳解

to call for help or complain about something when nothing is actually wrong
一切都很順利，卻要求提供協助或對某事抱怨

➲ Just ignore her. She is crying wolf again.
不要理她。她又在裝了。

➲ Don't cry wolf too many times or people won't come to help when you really need it.
不要常常裝可憐，否則當你真的需要幫助時，沒有人理你。

實用會話

A Officer! Please...help!
警官！拜託…幫幫我！

B Ma'am, are you ok? What's the emergency?
女士，妳還好嗎？有什麼急事？

A Nothing, I just need help carrying my bags up to my apartment.
沒有啦，我只是需要有人幫我把袋子提上去我的公寓。

B You shouldn't cry wolf like that. What would happen if while I was helping you, a real emergency occurred?
妳實在不應該像那樣假求助的。如果我過來幫妳時，有真的緊急情況發生了，該怎麼辦？

* cut class

蹺課

中英文詳解

to skip going to class in high school or university, usually without a good reason to do so (compare to play hooky)

高中生或大學生沒有正當理由卻不去上課。（對照 play hooky）

➲ I think I'm going to cut class today. I'm tired.
我想我今天會蹺課，我好累。

➲ Johnson, you are cutting class way too much. You are going to fail if you don't show up.
強森，你蹺課次數太多了。如果你再不來上課，我會把你當掉。

實用會話

A Where is Beth?
貝絲在哪裡？

B I think she and Lisa went to the beach.
我想她和莉莎去海邊了。

A Really? This is the fourth time they've cut class this week. They are going to get into trouble.
真的？這是她們這個禮拜第四次蹺課了。這下她們麻煩大了。

B I know. The teacher already called their parents.
我知道。老師已經打電話給她們的父母了。

A Oh, my! Beth's parents are going to be very angry with her.
喔，天啊！貝絲的爸媽會氣炸的。

MP3-8

D * dark horse

黑馬

someone, usually a political candidate, whose abilities, plans, ideas or feelings are pretty much unknown
某人（通常指選舉候選人）的能力、計畫、想法或感覺並不為人所知

➲ The winner of the presidential elections was a dark horse candidate until two months before the election.
總統選舉的當選人，是一位在選前兩個月，才被提名的黑馬候選人。

➲ It has been hard getting to know my son's girlfriend. She is a dark horse to me.
想要了解我兒子的女朋友一直都很困難。對我來說，她很陌生。

實用會話

A So, who are you going to vote for in the election?
那麼，這次選舉你會投票給誰？

B I don't know yet. I was thinking about voting for Jim Fisher.
我還不知道。我有想過要投給吉姆・費雪。

A Isn't he the dark horse candidate?
他不就是那位黑馬候選人嗎？

B Yeah, he is. But, he can't be any worse than the other candidates. Can he?
對啊，就是他。但是他總不會比其他候選人糟，是吧？

A Sure he can. You better find out more about him.
為什麼不會。你最好多瞭解他一點。

* dead end [n]

死胡同

【負面】

中英文詳解

an absolute ending point
死巷；困境

➲ When we reached the dead end, we had to turn around and go back the way we came.
當我們到了死巷子，必須迴轉然後走原路回去。

➲ I've been trying to solve this problem for days. But, I've reached a dead end. I don't know what else to try.
這幾天我一直試著去解決這個問題。但是，我已經用盡了方法。我不知道還有什麼方法可以試。

實用會話

A How's the research going? Are you close to being done?
你的研究進行得如何？快完成了嗎？

B Actually, no. I haven't made any progress on it for a month.
事實上，還沒。這一個月來我的研究沒有任何進展。

A Why? What's wrong?
為什麼？發生什麼事了？

B I hit a dead end when I ran out of money. Without it, there is no way to continue.
我遇到了瓶頸，因為錢用完了。沒有錢，研究就沒辦繼續進行。

A I'm sorry to hear that.
我很遺憾發生這種事。

* deadwood

無用的人或東西

中英文詳解

people or things that are no longer considered useful or needed

不再被認為有用或需要的人或東西

➲ The company is firing a lot of people. The president wants to get rid of all the deadwood.
這間公司正在大量裁員。總裁想要除去所有冗員。

➲ During the election the voters got rid of a lot of deadwood from the government.
選民在選舉期間幹掉了許多沒用的政府官員。

實用會話

A Blake, why are you throwing out all your stuff?
布萊克，你為什麼丟掉所有的東西？

B I'm not throwing out all of it, just the deadwood. I've got too much stuff and not enough space to store it all.
我沒有丟掉全部的東西，只有沒用的東西而已。我的東西太多，沒有足夠的空間可以收納全部。

A Wow... I don't think I could do that. I'm always afraid I may need something later. Hey... can I have that hat?
哇…我想我沒辦法像你這樣。我總是擔心以後我會需要用到某件東西。嘿…那頂帽子可以給我嗎？

B Sure, take it. It's yours. I've never worn it.
當然可以，拿去。這是你的了，我從沒戴過它。

* dirt cheap [i]

廉價

【非正式】

中英文詳解

extremely cheap
非常地便宜

➲ Mangoes are dirt cheap in the Philippines
在菲律賓，芒果很廉價。

➲ This car is dirt cheap. It makes you wonder if there is something wrong with it.
這部車是廉價品，所以你不禁會懷疑它是否有瑕疵。

實用會話

A Have you read the new Harry Potter book?
你看過最新的哈利波特了嗎？

B I want to. But, hardcover books are very expensive. So, I'll wait till it comes out in paperback.
我想要看呀，不過精裝本很貴。所以，我在等平裝本出版。

A I always buy my books at the discount store. Even the hardcover books are dirt cheap there.
我的書都是在折扣商店買的，在那裡即使是精裝本也很便宜。

B Really? Where is the store located?
真的嗎？那間店在哪裡？

MP3-9

* dirty work

苦活；違法勾當

中英文詳解

1.uninteresting or unpleasant work [c]
2. dishonest or illegal actions

1. 不有趣或令人不悅的工作【常用】

2. 不誠實或違法的行為

d

➲ My coworker is always traveling and meeting with clients, while I have to stay at the office and do the dirty work.
我的同事總是去外地出差與客戶見面，而我卻必須待在辦公室做苦活。

➲ When I got this job, the company seemed like a good place to work. Now I see that there is a lot of dirty work going on.
當我剛進來工作時，這間公司似乎是一個工作的好地方。現在我瞭解到有許多違法勾當正在進行著。

實用會話

A Pete. Can you help me with dinner tonight?
彼特，今天晚上你可以幫我準備晚餐嗎？

B Sure. What do you need me to do?
當然可以。你要我做什麼？

A I can make dinner, like I planned, but I have to leave right afterwards. Can you clean up for me?
我可以煮晚餐，就如同我原先的計畫，但是我煮完晚餐後必須馬上離開。你可以幫我收拾乾淨嗎？

B Sure, leave me with all the dirty work.
沒問題，你可以把所有的苦差事留給我。

A I know. I'm sorry. I promise to make it up to you.
我瞭解。很抱歉，我答應會補償你的。

* dressing-down

斥責

中英文詳解

a scolding or lecture about something one did wrong
因為某人做錯事情而引來的責罵或教訓

➲ My mom gave me a real dressing-down for breaking her favorite vase.
因為我打破了我媽最愛的花瓶，她好好地教訓了我一頓。

➲ The sergeant gave the recruit a dressing-down for not having his boots properly shined.
中士罵了新兵一頓，因為他沒有好好地把靴子擦亮。

實用會話

A What's up, Tom? You look annoyed.
怎麼了，湯姆？你看起來生氣。

B The vice president just gave my boss a dressing-down for the low sales figures this month.
副總裁剛剛訓斥了我老闆一頓，因為這個月的銷售數字很差。

A What? You don't think he deserved it?
什麼？你不覺得他活該嗎？

B No, that isn't it. It just bothers me that the vice president did it in front of everyone. I think he should have done it in private.
不，不是這個原因。只是副總裁當著大家面前罵人讓我覺得很困擾。我覺得他應該私下罵才對。

* dry run

彩排

中英文詳解

a practice attempt or rehearsal
嘗試練習或排演

➲ To make sure there are no mistakes, we should have a dry run before the ceremony tomorrow.
為了確保一切無誤，我們應該在明天典禮之前進行彩排。

D

➲ We found a number of problems when we had the dry run earlier. They will be fixed before the event starts.

先前進行彩排時，我們發現了一些問題。在活動開始前，這些問題會解決掉。

實用會話

A Mike, are you free on Friday night?
麥克，你星期五晚上有空嗎？

B Sorry, Jerry, I'm not. I have to be at the church for George's wedding.
抱歉，傑瑞，我沒空。我必須去教堂參加喬治的婚禮。

A I thought the wedding was on Saturday?
我以為婚禮是在星期六？

B It is. However, we are going to have a dry run on Friday night to make sure nothing goes wrong on Saturday.
是啊。不過，星期五晚上我們將會進行彩排，以確保星期六不會出差錯。

* dry up [i]

住口

【非正式】

中英文詳解

to become silent or stop talking

安靜下來或停止談話

➲ Please just dry up! I'm tired of listening to you.
請住嘴！我厭倦了聽你說話。

➲ The actor was so nervous that he dried up the moment he stepped onto the stage.
那位男演員非常緊張，一登台就忘詞了。

實用會話

A Brian, how was your trip to India?
布萊恩，你的印度之旅如何？

B It was great. I really found that the Indian people were very nice to me.
很棒啊。我真的發現印度人對我都很和善。

C Actually, the Indian culture requires that people are polite to strangers...
的確，印度文化要求人們對陌生人要有禮貌⋯

A Oh, dry up, Steven! I was talking to Brian. I wasn't talking to you.
喔，閉嘴，史蒂芬！我是在跟布萊恩說話，不是跟你。

MP3-10

eager beaver

做事非常賣力的人

中英文詳解

someone who is very enthusiastic; someone who works very hard
非常熱心的人；非常拼命工作的人

➲ The new associate was an eager beaver, arriving in the office before everyone else.
新同事工作非常拼命，總是第一個到辦公室。

➲ Our new volunteer is such an eager beaver.
我們的新志工非常熱心。

實用會話

A What are you laughing at?
你在笑什麼？

B I just find all the new freshmen amusing. The first month of school they are always so enthusiastic.
我只是發現所有的新鮮人都很有趣。開學的第一個月他們總是充滿熱情。

A Yeah, I know. They get up early so they can get breakfast and be perfectly dressed for their eight a.m. classes.
對啊，我瞭解。他們很早就起床、吃完早餐並且盛裝打扮去上早上八點的課。

B They are such eager beavers. Give them two months and they will be getting up five minutes before class, just like us.
他們是如此充滿熱情。不過，再過兩個月，他們就會像我們一樣，在上課前五分鐘才起床。

* eagle eye

目光銳利

中英文詳解

careful attention

非常專注

➲ The children played in the park under the eagle eye of the baby-sitter.
孩子們在褓姆的細心注意下在公園裡玩。

➲ The referee was known for his eagle eye during the games.
這位裁判因為在比賽時明察秋毫而聞名。

實用會話

A Did you get the information?
你取得資料了嗎？

B No, I tried, but I couldn't get it.
沒有，我試過了，可是還是不行。

A Why not?
為什麼不行呢？

B Ms. Glick, the boss' secretary, was there. I couldn't get it because of her eagle eye. She was watching me the entire time.
葛立克小姐，老闆的秘書，正在那邊。她的眼光銳利，我沒辦法拿到資料。她一直盯著我。

A Ok. I'll go keep her busy. You try again.
好吧，我會引開她。你再試一次。

e

* early bird

早起的鳥兒

中英文詳解

someone who gets up or arrives early, especially someone who gains an advantage by doing so

早起或提早抵達的某人，特別指因為這樣做而獲益的人

➲ I was the early bird this morning and got the first choice of bread at the bakery.
今天早上我很早起床，所以有機會在麵包店挑到我最愛的麵包。

➲ They were early birds and caught the first flight in the morning.
他們很早就起床了，所以趕上了早上的第一班飛機。

實用會話

A Good morning!
早安！

B Oh... Jonathan, good morning. I didn't expect to see you here. Usually I'm the first one in the office.
喔……強納森，早安。我沒想到你會這麼早來。我通常是第一個到辦公室的人。

A I have a lot of things to do today. So, I decided to be an early bird and get things started.

今天我有一堆工作要做。所以，我決定早起，好開始工作。

B Well, it's nice to have some company this early.

嗯，這麼早有人陪真好。

* expecting

[also: expecting a child]

懷孕

【也做：expecting a child】

中英文詳解

pregnant

懷孕

➲ Did you hear? Julia is expecting her first child.

你聽說了嗎？茱莉亞懷了第一胎。

➲ I just found out that Bart and Des are expecting again.

我剛知道巴特和黛絲又有了孩子。

實用會話

A You are not going to believe this!
你一定不會相信的！

B What? What's going on?
什麼？發生什麼事了？

A My mom just called me and told me she had some surprising, but wonderful news.
我媽剛打電話給我，告訴我她有讓我驚喜的消息。

B Yes? And? What was the news?
真的嗎？然後呢？什麼消息？

A She's expecting again! I'm going to have a baby brother!
她又懷孕了！我要有弟弟了！

* eye candy [i]

賞心悅目

【非正式】

中英文詳解

something, usually a man or woman, that is very good-looking

某物，外貌很好看，通常是男人或女人

E

➲ I saw some nice eye candy at the mall yesterday. One guy was gorgeous!
昨天我在購物中心看見了很養眼的人，有個男生長得很帥！

➲ The car is definitely eye candy, but it lacks good performance.
這部車看起來很漂亮，但是它的性能不好。

實用會話

A Chris, what are you doing here at the beach? Don't you have an exam tomorrow?
克莉絲，你在海邊做什麼？你明天不是有考試嗎？

B Yes, I just thought I'd enjoy the sunshine while I study.
是的，我只是想一邊唸書一邊享受陽光。

A Uh... Are you here for sunshine or for the eye candy?
嗯……，你來這裡是為了曬太陽還是為了讓眼睛吃冰淇淋？

B Ok... ok. I admit it. There are some hot looking guys around here. That is the main reason I came here to study.
好……好，我招了，這裡是有些很帥的猛男，這是我來這裡唸書的主要原因。

MP3-11

f

F * fair game

可抨擊的對象

中英文詳解

something that is acceptable to do, talk about, or attack

可以去做、談論或攻擊的事

➲ Being in the public eye makes you fair game for gossip.
身為公眾人物，讓你成為八卦的批評對象。

➲ When a celebrity does something wrong, journalists consider them fair game.
當名人做錯事時，記者會把他們當成批評的對象。

實用會話

A This makes me so mad!
這讓我很生氣！

B What does? The article you are reading?
什麼事？是你正在讀的文章嗎？

A Yeah. The reporter is saying some horrible things about my favorite candidate.
是的。這個記者針對我最喜愛的候選人報導了一些可怕的事。

B Hey, you know perfectly well. In an election, almost everything is fair game.
嘿，你知道的嘛，選舉時，幾乎每件事都會成為批評的目標。

* fall flat

[also: fall flat on one's face]

灰頭土臉

【也做：fall flat on one's face】

中英文詳解

to be completely unsuccessful
徹底失敗

➲ I don't know why, but my jokes always seem to fall flat.
不知道為什麼，我的笑話總是無法引起共鳴。

➲ When I gave my speech, I fell flat on my face. No one liked it.
我的演講完全不成功，沒有人喜歡。

實用會話

A Hey, Ian. How did the opening night of your play go?
嘿，伊恩，你的開幕之夜演出如何呀？

f

B It was horrible. The performance fell flat. No one seemed to like it.
很糟糕，表演徹底失敗，似乎沒有人喜歡看。

A Oh, no! That's terrible. What happened?
喔，不會吧！真糟糕，發生什麼事了？

B I have no idea. But, the audience didn't laugh at any of the funny parts. I guess they just weren't with it.
我不知道。在演到好笑的部分時，觀眾都沒有笑。我猜他們看不懂。

* fall short (of something)

〈某件事的〉短缺

中英文詳解

1. to lack enough of something;
2. to fail to achieve a goal [c]

1. 每件事的不足
2. 沒有達到目標【常用】

➲ By the end of the month I always fall short of money.
每到月底我總是缺錢。

F

➲ Unfortunately, the office fell short of our sales goal for the month.

很不幸地，本公司這個月並未達到預定的銷售目標。

實用會話

A (phone ringing) Hello?

（電話響）喂？

B Frank, this is Brian. Do you have a minute to talk?

法蘭克！ 我是布萊恩。方便說話嗎？

A Sure, Brian. What's up?

可以啊！ 布萊恩，有什麼事嗎？

B Well, I've been looking at this month's progress report. If we don't do something quickly, we are going to fall short of our production goal.

嗯，我剛剛在看這個月的進度報告。如果我們不快一點採取行動的話，恐怕無法達到目標生產量。

f

MP3-12

* fat chance [i] [n]

機率渺茫

【非正式；負面】

a very small chance or likelihood
機會或可能性很小

➲ Fat chance that my father will lend me the money I need to buy that car!
要我爸爸借錢給我買車根本不可能！

➲ You think she'll go on a date with you? Fat chance!
你認為她會跟你約會？不可能！

實用會話

A There's Jessica. I think she is wonderful. If I could just get her to go on a date with me.
潔西卡在那裡！ 我真欣賞她，如果可以跟她出去約會就好了。

B That won't happen. She's dating Joseph, remember?
那是不可能發生的事。她跟約瑟夫在一起，你忘啦？

A I know. But, I heard that they broke up last week.
我知道。可是，我聽說他們上禮拜分手了。

B Fat chance! They are very much in love. They are getting married in three months.
不可能！他們感情好得很，三個月後就要結婚了！

* fighting chance

勝算

中英文詳解

a good possibility, especially if every effort is made
經過努力獲得的成功機率

➲ He was seriously injured. But, he has a fighting chance of surviving.
他傷得很重，但是他仍有存活的勝算。

➲ If he can make a good impression at this meeting, he has a fighting chance of getting the account.
如果他能在這次的會議中建立良好的印象的話，我們得標的機會應該很大。

實用會話

A Do you think that she can win the election?
你認為她會贏得這一次的選舉嗎？

B If she can make a good impression on voters over the next two months, I think she can.
如果她能在接下來的二個月中，在選民心目中建立好印象的話，我認為她會贏。

A So, she has a fighting chance?
所以，她頗有勝算囉？

B Yeah, I think she does. The polls are close, but I think she'll win.
是呀，我覺得她有。現在民調結果很接近，可是我認為她會贏。

* final fling

最後一次機會做

中英文詳解

the last chance to do something, usually something enjoyable, before a major change in one's life

做某事的最後機會，通常指令人愉快的事，人們在一生重大改變之前做的事。

F

➲ Joan went out with her girlfriends to her favorite club for a final fling before getting married next week.

瓊安在下星期結婚前，要跟她的女性朋友去她最喜歡的俱樂部狂歡。

➲ Jack and Diane decided to have a final fling this weekend. Their baby is due to be born in two weeks.

傑克和黛安決定這個週末享受最後一次的二人世界，他們的小寶寶兩個星期後就要出生了。

實用會話

A I can't believe you are moving to the US. I'm going to miss you so much.

真不敢相信你就要搬去美國了，我會很想你。

B I'm going to miss you, too. But, the job is too good to give up.

我也會很想你，可是，這份工作放棄了很可惜。

A I know... Hey! Why don't we have one final fling this weekend before you go?

我知道……嘿！不如我們這個週末在你離開前去狂歡吧？

B That sounds great. I'd like that a lot.

好主意！我很想去。

f

* fine print

[also: small print] [n]

常被忽略的細節

【也做：small print；負面】

中英文詳解

important sections of a document that are often missed or overlooked, usually because of the small size of the print

文件中常常因為字體過小而被遺忘或忽略的部分

➲ You should always look at the fine print before you sign a contract.
簽約之前，別忘了要閱讀所有的細節。

➲ The car seems to be very inexpensive. But, if you look at the fine print, you can see it is quite expensive.
那輛車看起來好像不貴。但是你如果仔細看，就會發現它其實蠻貴的。

實用會話

A I should have listened to my dad!
早知道就該聽我爸爸的！

B Why? What happened?
為什麼？ 怎麼了？

A He told me to read the fine print before signing anything.
他叫我在簽約之前，一定要把所有的細節都看過。

B And?
然後呢？

A And, now I have to pay $20,000 to my employer for quitting before my contract is up.
然後，我現在因為在約滿前離職，得付我老闆二萬塊。

MP3-13

* flat broke

身無分文

中英文詳解

to have no money at all
完全沒有前

➲ I'm sorry. I can't go out with you, because I'm flat broke.
對不起，我不能跟你出去，因為我一毛錢也沒有。

➲ Did you hear? They say that Bill Gates is flat broke.
你聽說了嗎？據說比爾蓋茲破產了。

f

實用會話

A Are you going to go to see the movie with us?
要不要跟我們去看電影？

B I'd love to. I've wanted to see that movie for months. But, I'm flat broke.
我很想，我早就想看那部片子了。可是我一毛錢也沒有。

A Really? I thought you just got paid.
怎麼會？我以為你才剛領薪水。

B I did. But, I had to use all my money to pay my bills. I have nothing left.
是啊！可是當我付完所有的帳單之後，就什麼也沒剩了。

* forbidden fruit

禁果

中英文詳解

something or someone that is desirable but unobtainable, often because it is not allowed

通常指因受到禁止，而令人想得到的東西或人

F

➲ Ever since the doctor told Ken coffee is a forbidden fruit, he has had strong cravings for it.
自從醫生禁止肯喝咖啡後，他卻越來越想喝咖啡。

➲ Jody has a big crush on her teacher, but he is forbidden fruit and she can't date him.
裘蒂雖然暗戀她的老師，可是師生戀是禁止的。

實用會話

A Have you talked to Lucy lately? She says she's in love with her sister's husband.
你最近有和露西聯絡嗎？她說她愛上她姊夫了。

B I know. It's really crazy.
我知道，這真是太瘋狂了。

A I think she just finds him attractive because he is forbidden fruit. You know?
我覺得因為她不可能擁有他，所以她才會對他有意思。你懂吧？

B Hmm. You may be right. She didn't like him that much before he and her sister got married.
嗯，也許你是對的。在她姊姊結婚前，露西也沒那麼喜歡他。

* foul play

惡意；惡行

中英文詳解

illegal activity; bad practices (compare to funny business & monkey business)

不法行為；不道德的行為〈對照 funny business 與 monkey business〉

➲ The police suspect that her husband's death was the result of foul play.
警方懷疑她丈夫是遭謀殺致死的。

➲ There is some money missing from the company. It must be foul play.
公司有款項遺失，一定是被偷了。

實用會話

A Excuse me, Professor. I need to show you something.
抱歉，教授，我有些東西想給你看。

B What is it?
是什麼？

A I was grading these papers like you asked me. And, well, a lot of the students seem to have the exact same answers. It looks like some of them cheated.

我依你的要求改這些作業時，發現有很多學生的答案一模一樣。看起來有些人作弊。

B Hmm. You're right. There is definitely foul play here.

嗯，你說得對。這看起來的確像作弊。

* funny business [i]

搞鬼；不尋常之事

【非正式】

中英文詳解

illegal activity; bad practices (often: "there + be-verb + funny business going on;" compare to foul play & monkey business)

不法行為；不道德的行為〈常以 there+be 動詞+funny business going on 形式使用。對照 foul play (P75) 與 monkey business (P115)〉

➲ The silence in the room when she entered told the teacher there had been some funny business going on.

教室內鴉雀無聲，讓這位老師知道一定有不規矩的事發生。

➲ There is some funny business going on at my house. Money from my wallet keeps disappearing.
我住的地方一定有人手腳不乾淨，我的錢老是不翼而飛。

實用會話

A Ok... why are you guys so quiet? What have you done?
好啦…你們為什麼這麼安靜？是不是做了什麼事？

B Nothing, Mom. We are just playing.
沒有啊，媽媽。我們只是在玩而已。

A I don't think so. Whenever you two are quiet, you are usually up to some kind of funny business.
才怪！你們兩個要是安靜下來就是在搞鬼。

B Honest, Mom. We are being good.
真的啦，媽媽。我們很乖。

A Ok. But, if I find out you're lying, you will be in trouble!
好吧，要是被我發現你們騙我，你們就遭殃了！

*get fresh (with somebody) [n]

MP3-14

〈對某人〉毛手毛腳

【負面】

中英文詳解

to be extremely daring or impolite with someone, usually in regards to physical or sexual intimacy

對某人太過親密或無理，通常是指身體上的親近或性騷擾

➲ Charles got fresh with me the other night. He tried to kiss me without asking first.
查理斯前天晚上對我毛手毛腳，他企圖未經我的同意就親我。

➲ Josh has a habit of getting fresh with pretty girls.
賈許有對漂亮女生毛手毛腳的壞習慣。

實用會話

A Britney, how did your date with Craig go last night?
布蘭妮，昨晚跟葛瑞格約會如何？

B It was going really well until the end of the date.
直到約會結束前都滿順利的。

A Oh? What happened?
哦？發生什麼事了？

B He asked me if he could kiss me and I said yes. But, then he tried to get fresh with me. Instead of a nice kiss, he tried to stick his tongue in my mouth.
他問可不可以親我，我說好。可是後來他越來越放肆，不是禮貌性的吻，他竟然想把舌頭伸進我嘴裡。

* go bananas [i]

發瘋

【非正式】

中英文詳解

go crazy
發瘋

➲ What is wrong with the dog? He is going bananas.
那隻狗怎麼了？牠在發瘋。

➲ If my mother finds out I broke the window, she will go bananas.
如果我媽媽知道我把窗子打破，她一定會氣瘋了。

實用會話

A How long till we can go home?
還要多久才能回家？

B I don't know. All the flights out of the airport are canceled because of the storm.
我也不知道。所有班機都因暴風雨取消了。

A Ugh. I hope it is soon. Sitting here with nothing to do is extremely boring.
哎喲，我希望可以快一點。坐在這裡沒事做，實在很無聊。

B I agree. If we are here much longer, I'm going to go bananas.
我同意，如果我們還要在這裡等很久的話，我就要發瘋啦！

* go Dutch

各付各的

中英文詳解

to share the cost of something, usually a meal, with each person paying their own costs

分擔某件事的費用，通常是用餐時，每個人付自己的餐費

➲ If you want to go to the concert tonight, we need to go Dutch. I can't afford to pay for both of us.
如果你要一起去看演唱會的話，我們得各付各的。我沒錢買兩張票。

➲ Amy and I went Dutch at dinner last night.
艾美和我昨晚吃飯各自結帳。

實用會話

A How was your date with Kelly last night?
你昨天跟凱莉的約會如何？

B We weren't on a date. We are just friends.
我們不是在約會。我們只是朋友。

A But, you asked her out to dinner and a movie. That sounds like a date to me.
又吃飯又看電影哪像朋友，聽起來就像是約會。

B It was not a date. If it was a date, would we have gone Dutch?
那不是約會啦，如果真是約會，我們會各付各的嗎？

A Maybe, if you are cheap!
有可能，搞不好是你小氣！

* go overboard

太過於；汲汲於

中英文詳解

to do something to a greater degree than is necessary or reasonable

做某事超過需要或合理的程度

➲ Amanda usually goes overboard when she puts on her makeup.
阿曼達總是把妝化得太濃。

➲ My girlfriend is so afraid of making me angry that she goes overboard in doing nice things for me.
我女朋友很怕惹我生氣，所以她總是對我好過頭了。

實用會話

A Jonah, how was your trip back to the US?
約拿，回美國好玩嗎？

B It was good. But, I think I gained 10 kg.
還不錯。不過，我想我大概胖了十公斤。

A Yeah, you looked like you gained a little weight.
是呀，你看起來是有點發福的樣子。

B My mom was so happy to see me. She went a bit overboard making food. She made all my favorite dishes.
我媽媽見到我太開心了，她猛做我愛吃的東西給我吃。

A My mom is the same way. But, at least you had a good time.
我媽媽也是這樣，至少你玩得開心就好。

MP3-15

* green thumb

精於園藝

中英文詳解

to be good at growing plants
擅長栽種植物

➲ My aunt seems to have a green thumb. She can grow anything.
我阿姨還蠻精於園藝的，她什麼都能種。

➲ I love plants, but I definitely don't have a green thumb. Every plant I buy dies.
我很喜歡植物，可是我一定不擅於園藝，我買的盆栽都死了。

實用會話

A Hey, Jane, when do you start your vacation?
嘿，珍，妳什麼時候開始放假？

B Tomorrow... Oh, that reminds me. Can you take care of my plants for me while I'm gone?
明天……喔！這倒提醒我了，你可不可以在我不在的時候，幫我照顧我的植物？

A Uh... I guess so. But...
呃……應該可以。可是……

B What's wrong?
可是什麼？

A Well, I don't have the green thumb as you do!
我可不像妳那麼精於園藝喔！

* grey area

[also: gray area]

模糊地帶

【也做：gray area】

中英文詳解

a subject that is hard to define or put into one category; something that is neither good nor bad
很難定義或分類的議題；不算好也不算壞的東西

g

➲ Marketing of products is a grey area in the company. Both sales and product development handle it.
產品行銷在這個公司的定位不明，業務部和產品研發部都在負責。

➲ They couldn’t prove that he did it. So, his guilt remained a grey area.
他們無法證明這件事是他做的，因此他的罪名仍有待澄清。

實用會話

A Billy, what are you doing? Isn't it illegal for people to smoke marijuana?
比利，你在做什麼？抽大麻不是違法的嗎？

B Well, it is. Most people think it is ok if it is used for medical purposes. In fact, most police won't arrest you for it!
是啊！但大部份的人認為，只要是醫療用途就沒關係。事實上，大部分的警察都不會因此逮捕你！

A Wow. That is still very risky. You’d better be careful.
哇！那還是很冒險吧？你最好小心一點。

B I know it's a grey area. But, I'm willing to take the chance.
我知道這是模糊地帶，但是我願意冒這個險。

MP3-16

* halfhearted

心不在焉

中英文詳解

to be unenthusiastic about doing something

冷淡地做一件事

➲ John made a halfhearted attempt to play the game, since he wasn't concerned about winning.
約翰隨隨便便地打完這場比賽，因為他根本不在乎輸贏。

➲ Sally's halfhearted studying meant she just barely passed the test.
莎莉無心唸書意味著她剛剛通過了測試。

實用會話

A How did the game go yesterday?
昨天的比賽如何？

B We lost... 34 - 96.
我們輸了……34 比 96。

A What happened?
發生什麼事了？

B Everyone's effort was only halfhearted, since there was no way we were going to make it into the finals.
因為我們根本不可能打進決賽，大家就都心不在焉的。

A You should always play your best. No matter what!
不管怎麼樣都應該盡全力才對啊！

* hands down

輕而易舉

中英文詳解

easily; with little effort or opposition
容易地；不需要太多努力或沒有什麼反對意見

➲ She was the hands down choice for the best actress Oscar.
她絕對是本屆奧斯卡最佳女演員。

➲ Hands down, my favorite place to travel is southern France.
無疑地，法國南部是我最喜歡的旅遊景點。

實用會話

A I haven't heard the election results. Do you know who won?
我還沒聽到選舉結果，你知道誰贏了嗎？

B Yes. The opposition party's candidate was the hands down winner.
知道，反對黨候選人輕而易舉地贏了。

A Really? He was my choice. I'm glad he won!
真的？我也支持他，真高興他贏了！

B Yeah. He received almost 80% of the vote. None of the other candidates received more than 10%.
是啊，他得到近八成的選票。其他的候選人連一成的票都沒得到。

* hang on

稍等；抓緊

中英文詳解

1. to wait; to be patient
2. be ready for a sudden movement

1. 等待
2. 對突然的動作做好準備

➲ Hang on, will you? I'll be right there.
你稍等一下好不好？我馬上就過來了。

➲ Hang on! I have to make a U-turn. I missed the street.
抓緊喔！我得迴轉，車開過頭了。

h

實用會話

A Are you ready to land the plane?
你準備好要降落了嗎？

B Yeah, just hang on a minute. I'm checking the wind speed at the airport one final time.
好，再稍等一下。我最後確認一下機場那邊的風速。

A Ok... (over the intercom) folks, this is the captain. We'll be landing in a few minutes. Please hang on as this might be a bumpy landing.
好！（廣播）各位，這是機長，我們即將在幾分鐘內降落。可能會有些許顛簸，請旅客抓緊。

B Ok. I'm ready. Let's do it!
好，我準備好了，降落吧！

* high maintenance

難伺候的；注重外表的

中英文詳解

someone who requires a lot of attention; someone who spends a lot of time on their appearance

需要大量關照的人；花很多時間打理外貌的人

➲ Phillip's new wife is very high maintenance.
菲力普的新婚太太很難伺候。

➲ Jennifer spends hours on her hair and makeup. She's high maintenance.
珍妮佛花很多時間整理她的頭髮和化妝，她真是注重外表。

實用會話

A Mona seems to be a very nice girl. And, I can tell she loves you a lot.
夢娜是個很不錯的女孩，看得出來她很愛你。

B Mona is great. But... well, I'm beginning to realize that she's fairly high maintenance.
夢娜是不錯，可是……嗯，我漸漸發現她還蠻難伺候的。

A Really?
是喔？

B Yeah. She spends a lot of time on her appearance. And, if I don't constantly compliment her on her looks, she gets upset.
是啊，她花很多時間打理她的外表。而且，如果我沒有一直稱讚她的容貌，她就會不開心。

MP3-17

* hit bottom [n]

走到絕境

【負面】

中英文詳解

to reach the lowest or worst point

達到最低潮或最糟

➲ Our finances have hit bottom. We are now flat broke.

我們的財務狀況已經陷入絕境，我們破產了。

➲ I hit bottom about a year ago when I lost my car, my house, my job and my wife all within one month.

我一年前在一個月裡失去了車子、房子、工作和老婆的時候，真是陷入絕境。

實用會話

A So, where are we going to eat tonight?
今晚要去哪裡吃飯？

B Sorry. I can't go out.
抱歉。我不去了。

A Why not? You always like to go out to eat.
為什麼？你不是一直喜歡出去吃嗎？

B I know. But, I started a strict diet today. Yesterday, I hit bottom. I got on the scale and I now weigh 150 kg.
我知道。可是我今天開始節食。昨天我心情跌入谷底。我秤了體重，現在我有 150 公斤重了。

A Oh, wow. Well... let me know if I can help in any way.
哇，好吧……如果有需要幫助的地方儘管吩咐。

* holier-than-thou [n]

自以為是

【負面】

acting as if one is better than other people, especially in regards to behavior
自認為比別人傑出，尤其只行為方面

➲ Steven always has a holier-than-thou attitude. It really upsets people.
史蒂夫常常自以為是，令人很不悅。

➲ Jesse pretends to be holier-than-thou, but he has been in prison.
傑西老擺得一副瞧不起人的樣子，其實他坐過牢。

實用會話

A Oh, he gets me so mad!
喔，真會被他氣死！

B Who? The boss?
誰？老闆嗎？

A Yeah. He walks around here with that holier-than-thou attitude just because he's the vice president.
是呀，因為他是副總裁就在這裡走來走去，一付目中無人的樣子。

B I know. Everyone knows he wouldn't have gotten the job if he wasn't the president's brother-in-law.
就是嘛！所有人都知道，要不是因為他是總裁的小舅子，他也不可能坐上這個位子。

* hold water

合情合理

中英文詳解

to be correct or true; to be able to be proved (often neg.)

正確或真實的；可以證實的〈通常是負面意義〉

H

➲ Warren says he didn't take my money, but his excuses don't hold water.
華倫說我的錢不是他拿的，但是他的藉口不足以採信。

➲ The lawyer's evidence doesn't hold water. I think the man is innocent.
那個律師的證據不合情理，我認為那個人是無辜的。

實用會話

A Johnny, did you break this vase?
強尼，你打破花瓶了嗎？

B No, Mom, it wasn't me.
不，媽媽。不是我。

A Then who did it? You were the only one here.
那是誰？當時只有你在那裡。

B Well, you see, this rabbit hopped in through the window and...
呃，你看這隻兔子從窗戶跳進來，然後……

A Hold it, Johnny! That excuse doesn't hold water.
別說了，強尼！你的藉口根本站不住腳。

* Homebody

居家型的人

中英文詳解

someone who prefers to stay home, rather than go out to movies, clubs, bars, etc.

不喜歡去看電影、上舞廳、酒吧等等地方，反而喜歡待在家裡的人

➲ He rarely goes out after work. He's pretty much a homebody.

他在下班後很少出去，他很居家。

➲ My boyfriend and I are homebodies. We prefer to spend a quiet time at home rather than going out to bars and clubs.

我男朋友和我都是居家型的。我們寧可在家享受清靜也不願意到酒吧或舞廳玩。

實用會話

A Where is Steve? I thought he was coming tonight. What happened?

史蒂夫到哪去了？我以為他今晚會來。發生什麼事了嗎？

B He's at home with Chris. Ever since they started dating, he's been coming out less and less.
他跟克莉絲在家。自從他們開始約會後，他就越來越少出來玩了。

A I've noticed that. I don't think Chris likes to go out much.
我也注意到了，克莉絲不太喜歡出來玩。

B Yeah. The two of them have become a couple of homebodies.
對啊！他們倆都變成居家型情侶了。

* in season

MP3-18

[opp: out of season]

當季

【反義：過季】

中英文詳解

the correct time of year for something to be available to buy or hunt
某物在一年當中可買到或獵到的適當時間

➲ I love mangos. Unfortunately, they are only in season during the summer.
我愛死芒果了，可惜只有夏天才有。

➲ The hunters were arrested for shooting the deer. Deer are currently not in season.
那群獵人因為射殺鹿群而遭到逮捕，現在並不是補鹿的季節。

實用會話

A So, what are you going to have for dinner?
那麼，你晚餐想吃點什麼？

B Hmmm. I think I'll have the lobster. I love lobster.
嗯，我想吃龍蝦。我愛吃龍蝦。

A That sounds good. But, have you seen the price? It is really expensive right now.
聽起來不錯，但是，你看過價錢了嗎？龍蝦現在很貴呢。

B Wow! You're right. Why is that?
哇！你說的對，怎麼會這樣？

A Because lobster is not in season right now.
因為現在不是龍蝦的產季。

I

* inside joke

[also: standing joke]

私底下的笑話

【也做：standing joke】

中英文詳解

a subject that continually causes amusement among a group of people when it is mentioned.

總是令一群人發笑的話題。

➲ Jeff's habit of blowing air out of his mouth has become an inside joke among his friends.
傑夫吹牛的習慣已經成為朋友們私底下的笑話。

➲ Fannie's many different hairstyles often become inside jokes with her family.
芬妮多變的髮型常常成為家人的笑話。

實用會話

A Hey, John. Did you get the right salad dressing for your salad?
嘿，約翰。你用的沙拉醬是搭配你那盤沙拉的嗎？

B Yep. No tartar sauce this time. (Laughter)
是啊，已經沒有塔塔醬了。（大笑）

C Ah... I don't get it. What is so funny?
呃…不明白。有什麼好笑的嗎？

A Oh, sorry, Fred. It is an inside joke from a long time ago.
噢，不好意思，佛瑞德。那是一個內行人才懂的老笑話。

C Oh. Ok.
喔，好吧。

* in stock

[opp: out of stock]

有現貨

【反義：沒貨】

currently available, as with items in a store
現成可得的，如商店內的商品

➲ All of our holiday decorations are currently in stock.
我們所有的節慶裝飾品都有現成的。

➲ I'm sorry. The dress you want is not in stock. I'll have to order it for you.
很抱歉，妳要的那套衣服已沒有庫存了，我得再幫妳訂。

J

實用會話

A Sir? Excuse me.
先生？請問一下。

B Yes, ma'am. How can I help you?
是的，夫人。我能為妳效勞嗎？

A Your advertisement says that you have this TV in stock. But I can't find it on the shelves.
你們的廣告上說這台電視還有現貨，可是我在貨架上找不到。

B Oh. I'm sorry. We sold the last one this morning. We'll have more in stock on Friday.
喔！我很抱歉，今天早上我們已經賣出最後一台了。星期五還會進貨。

MP3-19

* just so

井然有序

中英文詳解

in perfect order; neat and tidy
有條有理；整齊又清潔

➲ Shirley's house is always just so.
雪莉家總是井然有序。

➲ Brandon likes to keep his desk just so. If you move something on it, he gets very upset.
布蘭登喜歡保持桌面有條有理；如果你動了桌上的東西，他會很生氣的。

實用會話

A So... Mom & Dad, what do you think of Patricia?
那……媽、爸，你們覺得派翠夏怎樣？

B She's seems very nice, dear. However... um... she seems a bit high maintenance.
她似乎不錯，親愛的。不過……嗯……她看來有點難伺候。

A Well, she does like to have things just so. But, I wouldn't say she's high maintenance.
喔，她確實是喜歡把東西打點得有條不紊，但是我不會用難伺候來形容她。

B Ok, dear. As long as you're happy, we're happy for you.
好吧，親愛的；只要你快樂，我們也會為你感到開心。

MP3-20

keep up

維持

中英文詳解

to be able to stay at the same level or speed as those around one

能和周遭保持同樣的水準或速度

➲ I went jogging with my roommate this morning. But, I had to stop after about 15 minutes. I just couldn't keep up with him.

我今天早上和我室友去慢跑，可是我跑了十五分鐘就停下來了。我就是趕不上他。

➲ I dropped the class because it was too hard. I couldn't keep up with all the work.

那堂課我不修了，因為太難了。我跟不上所有作業的進度。

實用會話

A Billy, I haven't seen you in class lately. Where have you been?

比利，我最近沒在班上看到你，你去哪了？

B Oh... I dropped out of that class two weeks ago.

喔……兩週前我退了那門課。

A Really? Why? I thought that was your favorite class.
真的？為什麼？我以為那是你最愛的一門課。

B It was. However, with working part-time and all the homework for the class, I just wasn't able to keep up.
曾經是。不過，我無法兼顧打工和那門課所有的作業。

* keep up

[also: keep up with the Joneses]

打腫臉充胖子

【也做：keep up with the Joneses】

中英文詳解

to try to have the same amount of money or possessions as someone else (Note: Joneses is the plural of Jones, a common family name in America).

試著擁有和別人相同的財富或地位（注：Joneses 是 Jones 的複數型，美國家庭常見的姓。）

➲ Peter is always buying things he doesn't need, just so he can keep up with the Joneses.
彼德總是買不需要的東西，他只是打腫臉充胖子。

➲ Always trying to keep up put me into serious debt.
總是愛裝闊，使得我陷入財務危機。

實用會話

A Did you notice that Luke bought a new car?
你有沒有注意到路克買新車了？

B Yeah. It seems like he buys a new one every year.
是啊，看起來他似乎每年買一輛新車。

A He does. His brother is a lawyer and he is always trying to keep up with him.
他的確是。他的哥哥是律師，而他總是想和他匹敵。

B But, Luke is only a teacher! How can he afford it?
但是路克不過是個老師！他怎麼負擔得了？

A I don't know. I think he is extremely in debt.
我不知道。我想他已負債累累了。

* keep up

[also: keep up with the times]

跟上流行

【也做：keep up with times】

中英文詳解

to stay current with fashion or what is going on in the world

跟著流行，或是最新形勢

➲ I decided to keep up with the times and buy all new clothes. My old ones were out of style.
我打算跟流行，買全新的衣服。我的舊衣服都已經退流行啦。

➲ I read the newspaper everyday. It is important to me to keep up.
我每天看報紙，迎合潮流對我很重要。

實用會話

A What in the world are you wearing? It is horrible!
妳穿什麼東西在身上呀？真恐怖！

B Huh? What's wrong with what I have on? It is very comfortable.
嗯？我的穿著有什麼不對嗎？穿起來很舒服啊。

A Maybe, but it is extremely out of style. You need to keep up with the times.
也許是吧，可是看起來非常老土，妳得跟上流行才行。

B I'm sorry. I'm not like you. I can't afford to buy new clothes every time fashions change.
很抱歉，我不像妳，我負擔不起跟著流行的腳步買新衣服。

* kill time

殺時間

中英文詳解

to waste time; to use up a period of time, usually while waiting for an event.
消磨時間；渡過某一段時間，通常指等待某事件的期間

➲ We walked around the airport to kill time before our flight left.
在班機離開之前，我們在機場附近走走打發時間。

➲ I should have used the time to study. Instead, I killed time watching TV.
我應該要利用那些時間來唸書，卻看了電視打發時間。

實用會話

A Hey, Jeff! What are you doing here? I thought you had a date with Sharon tonight.
嗨，傑夫！你在這裡做什麼？我以為你今晚跟莎朗有約會。

B I do. But, we aren't meeting till 8 p.m. and I had nothing to do. So, I thought I'd come to the mall to **kill time** until will meet.
是啊，可是我們約八點見，而我沒有事情做；因此我想去購物中心打發約會前的時間。

A Are you nervous about the date?
約會讓你緊張嗎？

B Very! I've wanted to go out with her for months.
非常緊張喔！我想和她出去已經想好幾個月了。

* laid-back

MP3-21

從容不迫的

中英文詳解

relaxed and easy-going;unlikely to worry or get upset

放鬆且不慌不忙；不怎麼擔心或沮喪

L

➲ I prefer to date a guy who is laid-back, rather than a guy who always worries.
我比較想和一個從容不迫的人約會，而不是憂心忡忡的人。

➲ Despite having a final exam in 10 minutes, David seems very laid-back.
儘管十分鐘內就要期末考了，大衛似乎非常老神在在。

實用會話

A Are you okay?
你還好嗎？

B Yeah, why?
好呀，怎麼了？

A Well, you are getting married in a half hour and you seem very laid-back. How can you be so calm?
再半小時你就要結婚了，可是看起來卻從容不迫的樣子。你怎麼能這麼冷靜？

B I know. It is weird. I thought I'd be really nervous right now. But, I'm just feeling relaxed.
我知道，這很奇怪。我以為我現在應該會很緊張，可是偏偏就覺得很輕鬆。

* landslide victory

大獲全勝

中英文詳解

to win by a large amount, especially in an election

大勝利，特別是用在指選舉

➲ The President enjoyed a landslide victory in the general election.
總統在普選中大獲全勝。

➲ The last time a candidate won a landslide victory was in 1954.
最後一次有候選人大獲全勝是 1954 年的事。

實用會話

A Did you hear? Jon Kelly won the election. I just heard the results on CNN.
你聽說了嗎？瓊 · 凱利贏了那場選舉，我剛從 CNN 聽到這個消息。

B Really? That's wonderful news. What was the final vote?
真的嗎？真是好消息。最後的得票數是多少？

A Kelly received 73% of the vote. Mr. Busk got 23% of the vote. And, the independent candidate got 4% of the vote.
凱利得到 73% 的選票，巴斯克先生得到 23%，而無黨籍候選人則只得了 4% 的選票。

B Wow... that was a real landslide victory for Kelly.
哇…凱利真的大獲全勝啊！

* loom large

赫然出現

中英文詳解

to be occurring in the immediate future, especially in regard to a problem, danger, or threat

特指即將發生的問題、危險或威脅

➲ Graduation is looming large, and I still don't have a job yet.
即將面臨畢業，而我還沒找到工作。

➲ The typhoon is looming large off the coast. It will hit within the next few hours.
颱風在海岸外突然成形，將在幾個小時後來襲。

實用會話

A Phew. I'm so glad that is over.
呼～真高興結束了。

B What? Your exam?
什麼？考試嗎？

A Yeah. As it began to loom large, I started to get more and more nervous. If I don't do well, I'll fail the course.
是呀，當考期逼近，我覺得越來越緊張；如果考不好，這門課就會被當。

B Oh. So, how do you think you did?
喔，那麼，你覺得你考得如何？

A I don't know. But, I did my best and now it's over.
不知道，但是我已經盡全力了，而且也結束了。

* lose face

顏面盡失

中英文詳解

to become less respectable or to lose status

變得不被尊重，或失去地位

L

➲ Having the boss yell at her in front of her coworkers caused Anita to lose face.
老闆當著安妮塔的同事面前吼她，讓她顏面盡失。

➲ Desmond lost face when he showed up for the meeting drunk.
當戴斯蒙醉醺醺的出現在會議時，他已顏面盡失。

實用會話

A Did you hear that someone is suing Brian? I can't believe he's going to have to go to court.
你聽說有人對布萊恩提出訴訟了嗎？我不敢相信他就要上法院了。

B Actually, Brian decided to pay the guy, rather than go to court.
事實上，布萊恩決定私下賠償，而不要鬧上法院。

A Why? He didn't do anything wrong.
為什麼？他又沒做錯什麼。

B Well, he figured it was better to lose some money than to lose face by going to court and having the trial in the papers.
嗯，他認為與其因官司纏身被報導出來而丟臉，不如花錢消災。

* lose heart

畏縮

中英文詳解

to lose one's courage or confidence

失去勇氣或自信

➲ Don't lose heart. I know you can reach your goal.

別氣餒，我知道你辦得到的。

➲ When Michael saw all the people waiting to hear him speak, he lost heart and got cold feet.

當麥可看到有這麼多人要聽他演講，他失去了信心而退縮了。

實用會話

A Gosh! I'll never get this straight!

天呀！我永遠沒有辦法弄清楚！

B Calm down and tell me what's up!

冷靜下來，告訴我發生什麼事了。

A I study and study and study these words. And, I finally think I've learned them. Then I go to use them and I can't remember how to pronounce them.

我讀了又讀這些生字，最後以為我已學會了，然後我試著使用這些字，但卻記不得它們的發音。

B Don't lose heart. Chinese is a difficult language. You'll get it soon enough.
別沮喪，中文不好學，你很快就會學會的。

MP3-22

money talks

有錢能使鬼推磨

中英文詳解

money has power; if you have money, you can get what you want
金錢就是力量；如果你有錢，就能得到任何你想要的

➲ The Smith Company offered me more money, so I will work for them. As they say, money talks.
史密斯企業提供我們更多資金，因此我將為他們效力。如他們所說：有錢能使鬼推磨。

➲ The senator got them to back down by offering them money - money talks.
那位參議員塞給他們一筆錢，使他們放棄—有錢能使鬼推磨。

A Why are you angry, Dawn?
你在生什麼氣，道恩？

B Well, I was going to buy a house. But, at the last minute, they said they couldn't sell it to me.
嗯，我本來要去買房子，可是最後他們卻說，他們不能賣給我。

A Why not?
為什麼不行？

B Some celebrity offered them more money for it. I hate to say it, but money talks.
某位名人付了更高的價錢。我討厭這麼說，可是，金錢萬能呀。

* monkey business [i]

暗中搞鬼

【非正式】

中英文詳解

irregular or unusual activities, often illegal ones (compare to foul play & funny business)

不正常的或少見的活動，通常是指違法的（對照 foul play 和 funny business）

➲ The children got involved in some monkey business at school and got into trouble.
孩子們在學校惡作劇，而且惹上麻煩。

➲ There has been some monkey business with the company's accounts.
公司的帳目已遭人暗中搞鬼。

實用會話

A Hello, dear. How was your day?
哈囉，親愛的。今天過得如何？

B Very interesting. When I got into work this morning, I found out my manager has been fired.
非常有趣，今天早上一進辦公室時，我就發現經理已經被革職了。

A Really? What happened?
真的？發生什麼事了？

B Well, apparently there was some monkey business between him and his secretary.
嗯，很顯然他和他的秘書有非法勾當。

MP3-23

* night owl

夜貓子

中英文詳解

someone who prefers to stay up late
喜歡熬夜的人

➲ Garrett is a real night owl. He usually goes to bed around 4 a.m. and gets up at noon.
蓋倫特是真正的夜貓子，他經常凌晨四點才睡，中午起床。

➲ I've always been more of a night owl. I do my best work at night.
我經常當夜貓子熬夜，我在晚上工作狀態最佳。

實用會話

A Is it all right if I call you later on tonight?
我今晚晚點打給你可以嗎？

B Sure. No problem.
當然，沒問題。

A Good. Thanks. When do you go to bed? I don't want to call too late.
很好，謝啦。你會幾點睡？我不想太晚打電話。

B Oh, don't worry about it. I'm a regular night owl. I usually don't go to bed till around 2 a.m.
喔，別擔心那個，我是夜貓子，通常不到凌晨兩點不會去睡。

* nobody's fool

精明者

中英文詳解

a sensible or wise person who is not easily fooled

一個敏感的或聰明的人，不容易被騙。

➲ Jackie is nobody's fool. She knows when someone is trying to cheat her.

賈姬是個精明的人，有人打算騙她時，總能一眼看穿。

➲ Don't lie to me. I'm nobody's fool.

別騙我，我可是很精明的。

實用會話

A Have you met the new project manager?

你見過新的專案經理了嗎？

B No. What is he like?

還沒，他怎麼樣？

A Well, he doesn't come across as very smart. But, actually, he's nobody's fool.

嗯，他看起來不聰明，但是事實上，他是個精明的人。

B Hmm. I knew somebody like him at my old job. You couldn't get away with anything with him around.
嗯，我以前的工作就有一個人很像他。只要有他在，什麼事都逃不過他的眼睛。

* nod off [i]

打瞌睡

【非正式】

to fall asleep
睡著了

➲ Bella nodded off during church on Sunday.
貝拉在教堂做禮拜時睡著了。

➲ After dinner on Thanksgiving my father usually goes into the study and nods off.
在感恩節的晚餐過後，我爸爸總是進書房打盹。

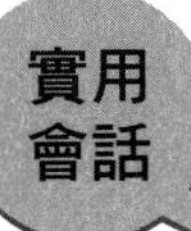

A How was your brother's wedding?
你哥哥的婚禮辦得如何？

B It was long and very boring. In fact, I nodded off during the ceremony.
既長又無聊。事實上，我在典禮上睡著了。

A Oh, no! Really?
喔，不！真的嗎？

B Yeah. That wasn't the worst part, though. I actually started to snore. My brother was quite upset with me.
是呀，其實那還不是最糟的部分。事實上我還打呼，我哥哥因此很氣我。

* no joke [i]

不開玩笑

【非正式】

a serious matter; to be serious
一件嚴肅的事；顯得嚴肅

➲ Having the teacher mad at you is certainly no joke.
讓老師對你發脾氣可不是鬧著玩的。

➲ You are 35 years old? No joking? Wow! You look a lot younger.
你三十五歲了？別鬧了？哇！你看起來年輕多了。

n

實用會話

A You wouldn't believe the night I had.
你不會相信那晚的事。

B What happened?
發生什麼事了？

A I took the wrong bus and ended up in Southeast DC.
我搭錯了巴士，而且停在東南特區。

B Oh... that is a dangerous area.
喔……那是個危險的地方。

A Yeah. That is no joke. Luckily, there was a taxi right there. So, I quickly got in and took that home.
是呀，那可不是開玩笑的；很幸運，剛好有部計程車在那，所以，我趕快搭上車回家。

* none too

不太

中英文詳解

not very; not at all

不太；一點也不

N

➲ You need to do laundry. The towels in the bathroom are none too clean.
你得洗衣服了，浴室裡的毛巾不太乾淨。

➲ When Josh walked into the office, he was none too happy. Apparently his car broke down and he had to walk to work.
當賈許走進辦公室時，看起來不太開心。看樣子他的車拋錨了，他只得走路上班。

實用會話

A How was your vacation?
你的假期如何？

B It was ok. Though I wasn't happy with the hotel.
還不錯。雖然我不太喜歡那個旅館。

A Why not?
為什麼不喜歡？

B Well, the first room they put us in was none too clean. The second room was cleaner, but had no air conditioner.
喔，他們為我們安排的第一間房間不太乾淨；第二間是很乾淨，卻沒有冷氣。

A Oh. That sucks.
喔！真糟。

* nothing but

只有

中英文詳解

only; just
只有，只是

➲ Alex buys nothing but brand name clothes.
愛力克斯只買名牌的衣服。

➲ Julia is on a diet and drinks nothing but water.
茱莉亞正在節食，所以只喝水。

實用會話

A Do you want to see a movie tonight?
你今晚想不想看電影？

B No. There is nothing playing right now that I want to see.
不，現在上映的片子沒有我想看的。

A Really? There are a lot of great movies out.
真的？有不少好片子上檔呢。

B I watch nothing but Meg Ryan movies, remember? And currently there are no movies with her in them.
我只看梅格萊恩的電影，記得嗎？而最近並沒有她演出的電影。

A Oh, yeah. I forgot.
喔，對喔，我忘了。

* nowhere near

遠不及，遠遠沒有

中英文詳解

not nearly
遠遠地

➲ We have **nowhere near** enough coal to last us the winter.
我們沒有足夠的煤炭能撐過冬天。

➲ Julian has **nowhere near** enough time to finish writing the book.
茱莉亞還差一大截的時間才能完成那本著作。

實用會話

A Aren't you going on vacation in a few weeks?
你這幾個禮拜內不是要去度假嗎？

B Yeah. I was supposed to go to Europe. But, now I'll probably just go to somewhere here in the US.
是的，我本來要去歐洲，但是現在我可能只在美國某個地方走一走。

A Oh... why the change in plans?
喔……為什麼改變計畫？

B Well, I had to get my car fixed recently. Now, I have nowhere near enough money to go to Europe.
嗯，最近我必須送車子去修理，去歐洲的錢我現在還差一大截呢！

MP3-24

*oddball

怪胎

中英文詳解

a strange person
奇怪的人

➲ Sheila is such an oddball. Have you seen the clothes she wears?
席拉是個怪胎，你有沒有看過她穿的衣服？

➲ People think I'm an oddball because I like to watch ballet.
大家覺得我是怪人，因為我喜歡看芭蕾。

A Brandy, have you ever had Professor Jones for American History?
布蘭迪，妳有沒有修過瓊斯教授的美國史？

B Yeah. He's a good professor. I think you'll like him.
有啊，他是個稱職的教授。我想你會喜歡的。

A I heard he was an oddball. Is that true?
我聽說他是個怪人，是真的嗎？

B He can be. But, the good part is his classes are always fun. You'll never be bored.
可能，但是，優點是他的課很有趣，不會讓人覺得無聊。

* off base

錯誤的

wrong or unrealistic
錯誤或不實際的

➲ The facts and figures quoted by the opposition party were way off base.
反對黨引述的事實和人物都不是真的。

➲ If you think I am interested in dating you, you are off base.
如果你認為我有興趣約你，那你就錯了。

實用會話

A You are way off base!
你弄錯了！

B What do you mean? My data is correct!
什麼意思？我的資料沒錯啊！

A No, it isn't. You claim that there were 300,000 people at the rally. But, there were only 30,000 people, at most.
不，有錯。你說集會有 300,000 人。但是，最多只有 30,000 人。

B That's not true!
那不是真的！

A Yes, it is. And, I can prove it to you. Look at this...
不，有錯。我可以證明給你看。你看這裡……

* off-color

下流的

中英文詳解

offensive, disrespectful, improper, or impolite
冒犯的，失禮的，不恰當的，或是無禮的

O

➲ Please don’t tell any more off-color jokes.
請不要再講下流笑話了。

➲ Off-color jokes or comments are not considered acceptable in this class.
課堂上不可以講粗鄙的笑話或註解。

實用會話

A Did you hear the joke about the farmer's daughter?
你聽過農夫女兒的笑話嗎？

B Yes, I did. And, I don't think you should be telling that joke, especially here at work.
有啊。不過我覺得你現在最好不要講，尤其是在工作的時候。

A Why not? It is very funny.
為什麼不行？很好笑啊。

B Whether you think it is funny or not is not important. It is very off-color and not appropriate for the workplace.
重點不是你覺得好不好笑，而是這個笑話很下流，不適合在工作場所講。

* old hat

老掉牙

中英文詳解

anything, except a hat, that is out of style, outdated or obsolete

除了帽子以外，任何退流行、過時或淘汰的東西

➲ You need a new computer. Your current one is old hat.

你需要一台新電腦。現在這台已經過時了。

➲ Wearing your clothes that way is old hat.

這樣穿衣服已經不流行了。

實用會話

A Can you believe my wife wants to get a job?

你能想像我太太想要找工作嗎？

B So? What is wrong with that? A lot of women work these days.

所以呢？有什麼不對嗎？時下很多女性都在工作啊。

A But, I think a woman should stay home, and take care of the house and kids.

但是，我認為女人該待在家裡相夫教子才對。

B You still believe that? That way of thinking is old hat.
你還信這套？那種想法早就老掉牙了。

MP3-25

* on target

如期完成

中英文詳解

on schedule; exactly as predicted
符合計畫；和預期完全相同

➲ We were on target for completion of the project until the typhoon hit.
颱風來之前，我們已經如期完成計劃。

➲ Our sales figures for the month of July were on target.
我們七月的銷售額如期達成。

實用會話

A So, how are the preparations for the big event coming?
那麼，這次盛大的活動準備得怎麼樣了？

B Well, we have three weeks to go and it looks like we are on target.
嗯，我們有三個禮拜的時間可以準備，我們會如期完成。

A That's great. I know you were worried about getting everything done on time.
太好了。我知道你們一直在擔心能不能準時完成。

B I still am. But, I think everything will be fine.
還是有點擔心。不過，我想一切都會很順利的。

* open-and-shut case

簡單明瞭

中英文詳解

something, usually a problem, that is simple and straightforward without any complications

通常指問題簡單易懂，一點都不複雜

➲ This is an open-and-shut case, Your Honor. I have sufficient evidence that my client didn't do it.
庭上，事情再明顯不過了。我有充分證據證明我的當事人沒有做這件事。

➲ It was an open-and-shut case. Austin was caught with the missing money in his pocket.
事情很明顯。遺失的錢在奧斯丁口袋裡找到了。

實用會話

A Detective Chen, what can you tell us about the investigation into the singer's death?
陳探長，那位歌手的死因調查得如何了？

B Well, there is no investigation, since it is an open-and-shut case. He killed himself.
這個嘛，沒什麼好調查的，事情太明顯了。他是自殺的。

A How can you be so certain?
你怎麼能這麼肯定？

B He left a suicide note stating his intentions to do so.
他留下一張紙條說，他想要自殺。

* open book

容易了解的人

中英文詳解

someone or something that is easy to interpret or understand

容易詮釋或理解的人事物

O

➲ Francine is like an open book. You always know what she is thinking.
法蘭欣根本藏不住心事。你一眼就看得出來她在想什麼。

➲ The council's plans are an open book. They are trying to save money, rather than do what is right.
會議的計劃一點都不難猜。他們想要省錢，卻不想做對的事情。

實用會話

A Tell me what is wrong.
告訴我怎麼了。

B What? Nothing is wrong. I'm fine.
什麼？沒事，我很好。

A No you're not. Your face is an open book. I know when something is bothering you.
不，你不好。你的表情說明了一切，我知道你有心事。

B Ok. I'm worried about my mother. She's going in for surgery today.
是這樣啦，我擔心我媽。她今天要動手術。

* out cold

不醒人事

中英文詳解

unconscious or in a deep sleep

沒有知覺或沈睡

➲ Last night I tripped, fell, and hit my head on the floor. I was out cold for at least a minute.
我昨天晚上跌倒了，頭撞到地板。我至少昏迷了一分鐘。

➲ After work Alex nodded off and was out cold for about 30 minutes.
愛力克斯下班後打了個盹，大概昏睡了半小時。

實用會話

A Did you feel the earthquake last night?
你昨天晚上感覺到地震了嗎？

B No. Was it a big one? When did it hit?
沒有。很大嗎？幾點開始搖的？

A It hit about 2 a.m. It wasn't too big. But, it was enough to wake me up.
大概半夜兩點開始搖的，沒有很嚴重。不過已經可以把我搖醒了。

B Oh, that's why I don't remember it. Once I go to sleep, I'm out cold till I wake up in the morning. It takes a lot to wake me up.
哦，難怪我沒有印象。我只要睡著，就會昏睡到早上才醒。要費很大的功夫才能吵醒我。

MP3-26

pipe dream

白日夢

中英文詳解

a wish or a goal that is impossible to achieve
不可能實現的願望或目標

- Jeff wants to be a rock star. But, I think it is a pipe dream. He can't sing or play an instrument.
  傑夫想要成為搖滾巨星，但我看他是在做白日夢。他不會唱歌也不會演奏樂器。

- I keep hoping I'll win the lottery. However, I know it is really no more than a pipe dream.
  我一直希望能中樂透。不過，我知道那不過是個美夢罷了。

實用會話

A So, if you could be anything you wanted, what would it be?
那麼，如果可以選擇，你想要當什麼？

B I've always wanted to become a great writer. You know, have one of my books on the bestseller list.
我一直想要當個偉大的作家。你知道，就是可以寫出一本擠進暢銷書排行榜的書。

A Well, what is stopping you? You can do that.
那你怎麼不去做呢？你一定可以的。

B No. It is really just a silly pipe dream. I don't have time to devote to writing.
不。那不過只是愚蠢的白日夢。我沒有時間專心寫作。

* pitch in

動手幫忙

中英文詳解

to help with something
幫忙做

➲ Tommy, would you please pitch in? We need to get this stuff packed by tonight.
湯米，你可以幫忙嗎？我們今晚前要把這些東西包好。

➲ Joannie, I need you to pitch in on this project. The deadline is soon and we are nowhere near done.
喬安妮，這項計劃需要你幫忙。期限快到了，離完成還差一大截。

實用會話

A Mom, are we ready to go yet? I'm getting hungry.
媽，我們準備好要走了嗎？我已經開始餓了。

B You know... we'd be ready quicker if you pitched in.
你知道…如果你動手幫忙會更快準備好。

A But, I don't want to help.
可是我不想幫忙。

B Well, then you can just sit there and be hungry. Because, I already told you, we aren't leaving till this place is cleaned up.
那麼你就只能坐在那邊餓著。因為我已經告訴過你，這裡沒打掃乾淨不能走。

A Ok, fine... I'll help.
好吧…我幫忙就是了。

*play along (with someone)

〈與某人〉假意合作

中英文詳解

to agree to cooperate with someone's plans; to pretend to cooperate with someone's plans (compare to play ball)

同意配合某人的計劃；假裝配合某人的計劃〈對照 play ball〉

➲ The man played along with the criminal until he had the opportunity to call the police.

那個人在找到機會報警之前，先佯裝和罪犯配合。

➲ I am playing a trick on Blake, so play along with whatever I say to him. Don't give me away!

我要跟布萊克開一個玩笑，所以不管我怎麼說都請合作一下。可別洩露了！

實用會話

A Are we going to have an anniversary party for Mom & Dad?

我們要幫爸媽辦結婚週年派對嗎？

B Yes. It will be in two weeks. But, don't tell them.
要啊。兩個禮拜後就到了，不過不要告訴他們。

A Why? Is it a surprise party?
為什麼？是驚喜派對嗎？

B Yeah. We are all pretending we forgot about their anniversary, so they don't know we are planning anything.
對啊。我們全部要假裝忘了他們結婚週年這件事，這樣他們才不會知道我們的計劃。

A Ok, I can play along. I'm good at keeping secrets.
好，我一定配合，我很會保密的。

* play ball (with someone)

〈與某人〉合作

中英文詳解

to cooperate with someone, often to get what you want in return (compare to play along)

和某人合作，通常會拿到謝禮〈對照 play along〉

➲ If you want to get a raise, you have to be willing to play ball.
如果你想要加薪，就要自願配合才行。

P

➲ You need to play ball with me or I may not help you.
你必須和我合作，不然我可能不會幫你。

實用會話

A I thought you said you didn't agree with the new dress code policy?
我以為你說你不贊成那項新服裝規定。

B I don't. But, I think making changes in the vacation policy are more important.
我是不同意。不過我覺得修改休假政策比較重要。

A So, you decided to play ball with management on the dress code, so you can get their support on the vacation policy?
所以你決定和管理部在服裝規定上合作，用來換取休假政策的支持囉？

B Yeah, that's right.
沒錯，就是這樣。

MP3-27

* play hooky [i]

跳課；蹺班

【非正式】

中英文詳解

to skip class or work, usually without a good reason to do so (compare to cut class)

蹺課或蹺班，通常沒什麼好理由〈對照 cut class (P44)〉

➲ It is such a beautiful day out. I think I'll play hooky and go to the mountains.
外面天氣真不錯，我想蹺課去爬山。

➲ Matthew doesn't like to work on his birthday. So, he usually plays hooky if it falls on a weekday.
馬修不喜歡生日那天還要工作。所以如果生日碰到上班日，他就會翹班。

實用會話

A Amanda, I didn't see you yesterday. Joe said you were sick
艾曼達，我昨天沒看到你。喬說你病了。

B Actually, I was playing hooky. Shhhh... don't tell anyone.
其實我是翹班啦。噓…要跟別人說。

A Really?
真的嗎？

B Yeah. After the weekend I had, I just couldn't stand the idea of coming in to work.
對啦。過了週末就不想上班了。想到要上班，實在受不了。

A I understand. Don't worry. I won't tell anyone.
我了解。放心，我不會跟任何人說。

* poetic justice

公正賞罰

中英文詳解

the unexpected but receiving of punishment or reward by someone who deserves it.

意外地受到該有的懲罰或獎勵

➲ The bank robber was caught after he dropped his ID at the bank. That's poetic justice.
那個銀行搶匪把身份證掉在銀行裡，就被逮補了。真是罪有應得。

➲ It was poetic justice that Sam got the promotion instead of Rob, since Rob tried to get him fired.
獲得升遷的是山姆而不是羅伯，真是再公平不過了；因為羅伯想要害他被解雇。

實用會話

A Hey, Brent, did you hear about what happened over at Larry's house?
嗨，布蘭特，你聽說了賴瑞家發生的事嗎？

B No, what?
沒有，怎麼了？

A Apparently a thief tried to break into his house by going down the chimney. But, he got stuck. Larry found him hanging there when he got home that night.
小偷顯然想要從煙囪溜進他家，但是被卡住了。賴瑞那晚回家時發現他吊在那裡。

B Oh, now that is poetic justice!
啊，那真是惡有惡報！

* poke fun (at someone)

嘲笑〈某人〉

中英文詳解

to make fun of someone; to tease someone

取笑某人；戲弄某人

➲ Stop poking fun at me. It is not nice.
不要再笑我了，這樣感覺很差。

➲ Alex and I have a great relationship. We are always poking fun at each other.
愛力克斯和我關係很好。我們經常互相取笑。

實用會話

A Jill, what's wrong?
吉兒，怎麼了？

B Jimmy was poking fun at me. I don't like it.
吉米取笑我，真討厭。

A Now, Jill, you tease him, too.
那麼吉兒，現在換你嘲笑他。

B I know. But, I don't like it when he makes fun of me.
我知道。但是我不喜歡他開我玩笑。

A Well, remember that the next time you want to poke fun at him.
下次你想取笑他時，請記住這一點。

* pull out

(of something or someplace) [i]

退出〈某事或某處〉

【非正式】

to leave or give up a place or situation
離開或放棄某個地方或某個情況

➲ Many people think the soldiers should pull out of Iraq.
很多人認為軍隊應該撤離伊拉克。

➲ This is too hard for me. I think I'm going to pull out of the race.
這對我來說太難了，我想退出比賽。

實用會話

A Jack, who are you going to vote for in the election?
傑克，你選舉那天要投票給誰？

B I'm pretty sure I'll vote for Jefferson Walters.
我非常肯定會投給傑佛森・華特斯。

A Oh, didn't you hear? He just pulled out of the election.
啊，你沒聽說嗎？他剛退出選舉了。

B Really? Oh no. Now who am I going to vote for?
真的嗎？哦，不會吧，現在我該投誰才好？

A I don't know. But, you better choose soon. The election is only 3 weeks away.
我不知道，不過你最好早點決定。再三個星期就要投票了。

MP3-28

* quite something [i]

棒極了

【非正式】

中英文詳解

something extremely nice or remarkable (the word "something" is always used in this expression)

某事物非常好或非常出色〈"something" 這個字在此一用法中都會跟著出現〉

➲ Joe & Chris' new house is quite something.
喬和克麗絲的新家真不是蓋的。

➲ The new chocolate dessert at San Marino's Restaurant is quite something. I love it!
聖馬利諾餐廳的新式巧克力甜點真是好吃。我愛死了！

實用會話

A Hey! Welcome back to Taiwan. How was your trip?
嗨！歡迎回來台灣。旅行還順利嗎？

B It was great! I really loved traveling in America.
真不錯！我好喜歡去美國旅行。

A What was your favorite part?
你最喜歡哪裡？

B I really loved being in the Midwest. The land is so flat you can see for miles. It is quite something!
我最喜歡中西部。陸地平坦無比，一望無際。實在棒透了！

A I've heard that it is beautiful.
我聽說那裡很漂亮。

MP3-29

R * rat race [n]

激烈競爭

【負面】

中英文詳解

the struggle for success, especially in business or one's career
為了獲得成功的奮鬥，特別用在商場或職場

➲ Philip is tired of the rat race.
菲利浦厭倦了無休無止的競爭。

➲ Suzy recently retired and got out of the rat race.
蘇西最近退休了，擺脫激烈競爭的日子。

實用會話

A For God's sake! I can't stand this!
看在老天份上！我受不了了！

B What's up?
怎麼了？

A I am so tired of the rat race - working long hours, trying to make enough money to pay bills that never stop coming...
這種激烈競爭的日子我快受不了了─長時間工作，只為了賺夠錢付那些永遠付不完的帳單……

B Well, what can you do? That is the way life is.
那你能怎麼樣呢？生活不就是如此。

A Nothing, I guess. But, sometimes I just want to give up.
沒事啦。不過有時候我真想放棄。

* red-handed

逮個正著

中英文詳解

to be caught doing something wrong
做壞事當場被抓到

➲ They caught the bank robber red-handed. He had the stolen money in his pockets.
他們當場抓到那個銀行搶匪。他把偷來的錢放在口袋。

➲ My mom knows I've been eating the cookies. She caught me red-handed with one in my mouth.
我媽知道我一直吃餅乾吃個不停。我放一塊在嘴裡時剛好被她逮個正著。

實用會話

A I haven't seen Bob today. Do you know where he is?
我今天沒看到包伯。你知道他在哪裡嗎？

B They fired him yesterday.
他們昨天把他炒魷魚了。

A Did they finally discover that he's been stealing office supplies?
他們終於發現他一直在偷辦公室用品了嗎？

B Yes. They caught him red-handed in the storeroom, stuffing notepads into his bag.
沒錯。他在儲藏室把筆記本塞進袋子時，被他們逮個正著。

r

* red tape

繁文縟節

中英文詳解

extremely complex, often difficult, rules and procedures, especially in government

非常複雜、往往又很困難的規則和程序，特別指官僚體制。

➲ Because of all the red tape, it took Richard two months to get the permit to build his house.

一大堆繁文縟節，讓理查花了兩個月才得到自行建屋的批准。

➲ Applying for a student visa in the United States requires going through a lot of red tape.

在美國申請學生簽證需要經過一大堆繁瑣的手續。

實用會話

A So, did you get your visa yet?

那麼你拿到簽證了嗎？

B Not yet. I'm still waiting for them to send it to me.

還沒有。我還在等他們寄來給我。

A Really? But, you've been waiting for it for at least two months.

真的嗎？但是你至少已經等兩個月了。

B I know. It is frustrating. And, I just got a letter saying I have to come in and deal with more red tape!
我知道，真是讓人覺得無力。我居然還收到一封信，叫我要去那裡辦更多繁人手續！

* ring true

像真的一樣

中英文詳解

to sound or seem true (often neg.)
聽起來或看起來像真實的（通常是負面意義）

➲ Jim's excuse for being late doesn't ring true.
吉姆遲到的理由聽起來不像是真的。

➲ Ok. Your reason for missing the deadline rings true. So, I'll accept it and give you more time.
好。你沒有趕上最後期限的理由聽起來不像是假的。我相信你説的話，會給你更多時間。

實用會話

A I thought you had a date with Sophie tonight?
我以為你今晚要和蘇菲約會。

B I did. But, she called and said she had to go help her mother at home.
沒錯。但是她打電話給我，跟我說她必須在家幫她媽媽的忙。

A You seem worried. Do you think she was lying to you?
你好像有點擔心。你覺得她在騙你嗎？

B Yeah. I do. I just can't explain it. Something about her reason just doesn't ring true.
是啊，但我說不上來。她的理由聽起來就不樣是真的。

* road hog [i]

路霸

【非正式】

中英文詳解

someone who drives carelessly or selfishly, acting as if they own the road
開車不小心或自私的人，好像路是他們家的一樣

➲ Look at that guy driving in the middle of the road. What a road hog!
看看那個把車開在路中央的傢伙。真是路霸！

R

➲ My cousin is such a road hog. He drives like he is the only one on the road.

我的表哥老像路霸，開車時好像整條路只有他一個人在開一樣。

實用會話

A Excuse me, ma'am. Are you alright?

對不起，太太。你還好嗎？

B Yes. Thanks, Officer. I'm fine. But, I'm afraid my car's not.

是的，謝謝你長官，我很好。不過我擔心我的車子可能不太好。

A What happened?

怎麼了？

B Well, I was starting to go through the intersection when a road hog made a left turn in front of me.

嗯，我正要過十字路口，結果有個路霸在我面前左轉。

A If you give me the type of car it was, I'll put out an alert.

告訴我是哪一輛車，我會通報上去。

* rough it [i]

過得很辛苦

【非正式】

中英文詳解

to live in simple or uncomfortable conditions

在沒有一般便利的和舒適的條件下生活

➲ We had to rough it while our house was being renovated since we had no water or electricity for two weeks.
房子需要整修，會有兩個星期沒水沒電，我們得忍耐一點過。

➲ The boy scouts spent a weekend roughing it in the woods.
童子軍在森林裡辛苦地渡過一個週末。

實用會話

A Kyle, do you want to go away with us this weekend?
凱爾，你這個週末要和我們一起去嗎？

B Where are you going?
你們要去哪裡？

Ⓐ We are going to go camping at the national park. It will be just us, the sleeping bags, and the tents.
我們要去國家公園露營。除了我們幾個，就只有睡袋和帳篷。

Ⓑ Uh... I don't think so. My idea of roughing it is to go without my DVD player for 24 hours.
嗯…我想我不去了。我只要想到離開我的 DVD 播放機 24 小時就覺得很辛苦了。

MP3-30

same difference [i]

差不多

【非正式】

the difference between two or more things is so small that it is not important
兩個以上的東西之間的差別，小到根本微不足道。

➲ I don't know which digital camera to buy. Oh well, I guess it is the same difference!
我不知道該買哪一台數位相機。真是的，看起來根本沒有什麼差別！

➲ Should I go on a date with Cindy or Patty? Same difference, I guess. They are both nice and cute.
我應該約辛蒂還是派蒂？我想都差不多，她們兩個都很不錯也很可愛。

實用會話

A Excuse me. Can I ask you a question?
對不起。我可以問你一個問題嗎？

B Sure. How can I help you?
當然。有什麼需要效勞的地方嗎？

A You are very tall. Are you 200 cm tall?
你看起來很高，有 200 公分嗎？

B No, I'm only 198 cm tall.
沒有，我只有 198 公分高。

A Oh, same difference!
哦，差不多啦！

* see things

眼誤；眼花

中英文詳解

to imagine one sees something or someone that isn't there

想像能看見不存在的東西或人

A You couldn't have seen your mother. She's been dead for two years. You must have been seeing things.
你不可能看到你媽媽，她已經去世兩年了，你八成是看錯了。

B When Justin walked into the room, I thought I was seeing things. He was supposed to be in Europe.
當我看到賈斯汀走進房間時，我以為是我眼花了，他應該在歐洲才對。

實用會話

A Did Ross tell you what he saw last night?
羅斯告訴過你他昨晚看到什麼了嗎？

B He told me he saw a UFO. Is that what he told you?
他說他看到飛碟。他也是這麼跟你說的嗎？

A Yeah. He said it flew over his house twice. Do you believe him?
是啊，他說飛碟飛過他家兩次。你相信他的話嗎？

B No way. I think he was either dreaming or just seeing things. There are no such things as UFOs.
才不呢。我想他不是在作夢就是眼花了。不可能有飛碟這種東西的。

* sit tight

稍待

中英文詳解

to wait, usually patiently (one does not need to be sitting)

通常指耐心地等待（並不是真的請某人坐下）

➲ Just sit tight and I'll have that money for you in a minute.
請稍候，我待會拿錢給你。

➲ Brian, sit tight. We'll go to McDonald's after I'm done making this phone call.
布萊恩，稍待一下。等我打完這通電話我們就去麥當勞。

實用會話

A Dad, are we there yet?
老爸，我們快到了嗎？

B I told you we'll be there in about 20 minutes.
我告訴過你大概再過二十分鐘就到了。

A But, I have to go to the bathroom.
但是我想上廁所。

B Julia, just sit tight and try not to think about it. We'll be there before you know it. Okay?
茱莉亞，再忍一下就好，儘量別去想這檔事。我們來得及的，好嗎？

A Okay... Okay...
好吧……好吧……

* sitting duck [n]

容易被攻擊的目標

【負面】

someone or something in a position that is easily attacked
指某人或某事處於容易被攻擊的情勢之中

➲ The old lady was a sitting duck for thieves. She lived alone and often forgot to lock her door.
那位老太太很容易被偷，獨居的她經常忘了鎖門。

➲ The last people to be hired are usually sitting ducks if the company has to reduce the size of the staff.
當公司必須裁員時，新進員工總是岌岌可危。

實用會話

A I can't believe some of the things the newspapers print about celebrities.
我不相信報紙上那些關於名人的報導。

B Like what?
比如說？

A This article talks all about the sex life of the actor in that new movie. It is horrible the kinds of things they are saying.
這篇報導談論那部新片中演員的性生活，提到的事都很可怕。

B Well, when you are celebrity, you are a sitting duck for that kind of gossip.
嗯，如果你是名人的話，你是逃不過八卦的。

* sixth sense

第六感

中英文詳解

an imagined ability to know things not perceivable by the five senses - sight, smell, hearing, taste, touch
一種非經由五官而察覺事物的能力。

S

➲ Patty claims to have a sixth sense about the future. But, I don't believe her.
佩蒂宣稱她擁有預知未來的第六感，可是，我並不相信。

➲ My sixth sense told me not to trust him. And, it was right. He tried to steal my money.
我的第六感警告我不能相信他，事實也是如此，他企圖偷我的錢。

實用會話

A You know that accident on Main Street yesterday afternoon?
你知道昨天下午在大街上發生的意外嗎？

B Yes. I read about it in the newspaper. It was horrible.
我知道，我在報紙上看到這則報導。太可怕了。

A Would you believe that I was almost in it?
你相信我差一點也捲入其中嗎？

B No way. What happened?
怎麼可能？發生什麼事了？

A My sixth sense told me not to go down Main Street and so I took Lombard Road instead.
我的第六感告訴我不要走大街，因此我改走倫巴德路。

S

MP3-31

* sleep in

賴床

中英文詳解

to sleep late

晚起

➲ On Saturday mornings I usually like to sleep in till at least 11 a.m.
每逢星期六上午，我經常睡到十一點才醒。

➲ Since school was closed today, I got to sleep in. It was so nice.
既然學校今天放假，我可以睡晚些。太棒了！

實用會話

A Good Morning!
早安！

B Huh? Oh... good morning! What time is it?
啊？喔……早！現在幾點啦？

A It's about 10:30 a.m.
大概十點半囉。

B What? Why didn't you wake me? I'm really late for work.
什麼？你怎麼沒叫我？我上班遲到了啦！

A No you're not. They called earlier. The office is closed because there is no power in the building. So, I let you sleep in.
不，你並沒有遲到，他們稍早來過電話；公司因為停電關閉了，所以我才讓你睡到這麼晚。

* small fry [i]

小鬼頭；微不足道

【非正式】

中英文詳解

1. children [c]
2. unimportant things or people

1. 毛頭小子【常用】
2. 微不足道的事或人

➲ Someone go get the small fry. It is time to open the Christmas presents.
誰去把小鬼頭們找回來，我們差不多該打開耶誕禮物了。

➲ Sometimes politicians treat the people they serve as just small fry.
有時候，政客們不把他們的選民當一回事。

實用會話

A Wow... there are a lot of kids running around the mall today.
哇……今天有好多小朋友在購物中心跑來跑去。

B Yeah. It is a school holiday today, so they all have the day off.
是啊，今天是假日，所以他們全都放假。

A I wish I had known there were going to be so many small fry here today. I wouldn't have come.
要是我知道今天會有這麼多小鬼頭，我就不會來啦。

B That's right. I forgot. You don't like kids, do you?
對喔，我忘了，你很討厭小朋友的，是吧？

* small-time

[opp: big-time]

小規模的；無足輕重的

【反義：big-time】

中英文詳解

small; unimportant
小型的；不重要的

S

➲ Our coffee shop is only a small-time business. It does ok. But, it can never compete with places like Starbucks.
我們的咖啡屋只是小本生意，經營還可以，沒有辦法和星巴克之類的咖啡屋匹敵。

➲ That's a small-time issue. I don't think we need to consider it.
那只是個小問題，我不認為我們有討論它的必要。

實用會話

A Hey, I hear that someone is going to open up another bookstore down the street.
嘿！我聽說這條街上有另一家書店要開幕。

B Yeah. I heard that, too.
嗯，我也聽說了。

A Do you think they'll have an effect on your sales figures?
你覺得他們是否會影響你的銷售量？

B Maybe at the beginning. But, from what I understand, they will only be a small-time store. So, they shouldn't affect us too much.
一開始也許會，不過，據我所知，他們只是個小規模的書店。所以，應該不會對我們有太大的影響。

* smooth sailing

輕而易舉

中英文詳解

progress that has been made without any problems or difficulties

過程沒有遭遇問題或困難

➲ Redecorating our house was smooth sailing from the beginning to the end of the project.
我們房子的重新裝潢從頭到尾都十分順利。

➲ Until the divorce, my life had been smooth sailing.
自離婚後，我的生活變得平順。

實用會話

A Hi, Greg. How's the project going?
嗨！克雷格。計畫進行得怎麼樣了？

B Well, we had some problems during the design process. The client kept making changes in what they wanted.
嗯，在設計的過程方面出了些差錯。客戶的要求一直在變。

A I'm sorry to hear that.
我很遺憾聽到這種事。

B But, now that the project is in production, it looks like smooth sailing from this point on.
但是現在計畫已經進入生產過程了，目前看來接下來的一切都很順利。

* squeak by [i]

勉強通過

【非正式】

中英文詳解

1. to barely manage [c]
2. to just get by someone or something

1. 勉強能應付過去【常用】
2. 剛好可以通過～

➲ I think I have enough food to squeak by until I can go to the supermarket on Saturday.
我想我還有足夠的食物，可以撐到星期六去超市為止。

➲ The bus was almost blocking the road, but I just squeaked by.
這部巴士幾乎堵住了整條路，可是剛剛好夠我通過。

實用會話

A How are your finances, Son? Are you on budget?
兒子啊，你的收入還可以嗎？有沒有財務危機啊？

B It's going ok. I think I have just enough money to squeak by till my next paycheck.
還好啦！我想我省點用剛好可以撐到下一個領薪日。

A Well, if you need any money, your mother and I are happy to help.
嗯，如果你需要錢的話，你媽媽和我都很樂意幫你。

B I appreciate that, Dad. But, I really want to try to do this on my own.
多謝啦！老爸。但是我真的想靠自己。

* stand corrected

認錯

to admit that one has made a mistake
承認自己犯了錯

➲ I realize now that I made a mistake. I stand corrected.
我現在知道我做錯了，我接受指正。

➲ Joe, you are right. Our data is wrong. We stand corrected.
喬，你是對的。我們的資料有錯，我們會更正的。

S

實用會話

A So, in conclusion... if we use this sales strategy, we should be able to increase our profits by 20%.
所以，結論是……如果我們採用這個銷售策略，應該可以提高約 20%的利潤。

B Excuse me, Bob? But, shouldn't the figure on line 4 be $24,000? That means the increase will only be 18%
包伯，抱歉打斷一下。但是在第四項的數據是兩萬四嗎？那代表只有 18%的獲益。

A You are right, Eileen. I'm not sure how I missed that mistake. I stand corrected. Thanks for pointing that out.
妳是對的，伊蓮。不知為何我漏了這一項，我知道錯了，感謝你把它指出這個錯誤。

B No problem.
不客氣。

MP3-32

* standstill

停頓

中英文詳解

to stop, temporarily or permanently
暫時或永久的休止

➲ Because of the accident, traffic was at a standstill.
由於那場交通意外，交通一度中斷。

➲ The scream in the night brought everyone to a standstill.
晚上那聲尖叫令所有人都停下來。

實用會話

A Hi, dear. I heard on the news that a typhoon hit Taiwan yesterday. Are you ok?
嗨，寶貝，我聽新聞說昨天有颱風過境台灣，你還好吧？

B We are fine, Mom. It hit harder in southern Taiwan.
我們都好，媽，南台灣比較嚴重。

A Was there any damage in Taipei?
台北有什麼災情嗎？

B Minor. Though work came to a standstill when the electricity went out at the office.
不嚴重。不過公司停電後，全部的工作都停擺了。

* stay put [i]

保持原狀

【非正式】

中英文詳解

not to move; to stay where one is

待在原地不動

➲ Just stay put. I'll be back in a minute.
留在原地，我馬上回來。

➲ This poster never wants to stay put. It keeps coming off the wall.
這張海報一直無法貼牢，它老是從牆上掉下來。

實用會話

A I hope everyone saved room for dessert. I made a cake and two pies. Plus, we have ice cream.
我希望大家還有胃口吃點心，我做了一個蛋糕和兩個派。此外，還有冰淇淋呢。

B Oh, wow, that is a lot. Let me help you get it all.
哇！這麼多，讓我幫妳端出來。

A Now you stay put. You are a guest. You just sit there and relax. I can get them.
好好坐著，你是客人，坐著放鬆一下，我可以自己搞定。

B Are you sure? I don't mind helping.
妳確定？我不介意幫忙的。

* stood up [n]

放鴿子

【負面】

中英文詳解

to have someone you are meeting not show up; usually said in regards to a date.

和別人約好卻被爽約；通常針對約會而言

➲ Jenna is very upset. She went on a date last night and got stood up.
珍娜非常沮喪，她昨晚赴約，結果被放了鴿子。

➲ Don't forget we have a meeting at 4:00 tomorrow. Don't stand me up like you did the last time.
別忘了我們約好明天四點喔，別再像上次一樣放我鴿子。

實用會話

A Sally...How are you?
莎莉……妳還好嗎？

B I am very annoyed with you. That is how I am.
我在生你的氣，那就是我現在的感覺。

A Huh? Why? What did I do?
嗯？為什麼？我做了什麼嗎？

B You stood me up last night. We had a date at the Waldorf! Remember?
你昨晚放了我鴿子。我們約好在渥多福見面的！想起來了嗎？

A Oh, no! I'm so sorry! I completely forgot.
喔，不！我很抱歉！我完全忘了這回事。

* straight out [i]

直截了當

【非正式】

honestly or directly
誠實地或直接地

➲ Wendy really hurt my feelings. She told me straight out she thought I was ugly.
溫蒂真的傷了我的感情，她毫不隱瞞地說我很醜。

➲ Ivy told John straight out that she didn't want to marry him.
艾薇直截了當地告訴約翰，她不想嫁給他。

實用會話

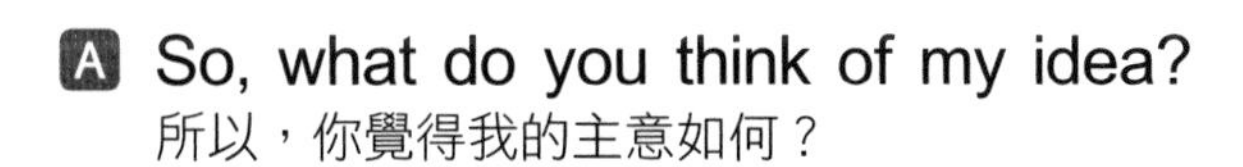

A So, what do you think of my idea?
所以，你覺得我的主意如何？

B Do you want an honest answer?
你要我誠實回答嗎？

A Of course, tell me straight out what you think. I value your opinion.
那當然，直接說出你所想的，我很重視你的意見。

B Well... I think your idea sucks. There is no way that it can work.
嗯……我認為你的主意很爛。那行不通的。

* suit oneself [i]

自便

【非正式】

中英文詳解

to do what one wishes
隨自己的意願去做

➲ You can stay here or find another place to wait. Suit yourself.
你可以留在這，或者在其他地方等，隨你便。

S

➲ My husband said he didn't care if I got a job or stayed home. He told me to suit myself.
我丈夫說他不在乎我有工作，或是閒居在家，他說隨我決定。

實用會話

A Hi, Blake. How are you?
嗨！布萊克。你好嗎？

B Good. Thanks. So... why are you sitting on the front porch?
很好，謝啦。那……為什麼你要坐在玄關？

A Sharon said that I should sit here and wait for her. We have a date, but she's running a little late.
莎朗叫我坐在這兒等她。我們約好了，可是她有點遲到。

B You are welcome to come into the house. It's up to you. Suit yourself.
你可以進屋坐坐，你決定，請自便。

* sweet nothings

甜言蜜語

中英文詳解

affectionate but unimportant words spoken to someone you love
說給情人聽的深情卻不重要的話

➲ John is always whispering sweet nothings into Sheila's ear.
約翰總是在希拉的耳畔情話綿綿。

➲ I want a man who has more to say than just a bunch of sweet nothings.
我要一個不是只會說花言巧語的男性。

實用會話

A You and Sean seem to be getting really close.
妳和尚恩看起來真的很親蜜喔。

B Yeah. We've been having a really good time together. The relationship is going pretty well... but... .
嗯，我們一同渡過很愉快的時光，感情變得很好……可是……。

A But what?
可是什麼？

B He never wants to talk about anything important. Most of the time he just wants to tell me a bunch of sweet nothings.
他從未說過一件正經事，大多數的時間他只想對我說一堆甜言蜜語。

MP3-33

* tag along [i]

尾隨

【非正式】

中英文詳解

to go along with or follow someone, usually when not invited

和某人作伴或跟隨著某人，大多是在對方不情願的情況下

➲ My little brother always used to tag along whenever my friends and I would go out.
每當我和朋友要出門的時候，我弟弟總是跟著我。

➲ Do you mind if I tag along? I have nothing to do tonight.
介意我跟著你嗎？我今晚閒著沒事。

實用會話

A Hey, guys! What's up?
嘿，大夥們！去哪？

B Uh... Joy and I were just going to see a movie.
呃……喬伊和我正要去看電影。

A Cool! I haven't been to a movie in a long time. Which one are we going to see?
酷！我好久沒看電影啦，你們要看哪一部？

B Daniel. We... uh... are on a date. We don't really want you to tag along. Okay? Sorry.
丹尼爾，我們……呃……我們正在約會，不太希望你跟著我們，好嗎？抱歉了。

* talk shop

三句不離本行

中英文詳解

to talk about business matters someplace where it is inappropriate, like at a social event

在不恰當的場合洽商，比如說社交場合。

➲ It doesn't matter where they are; Joe & Dylan are always talking shop.
不論喬和達倫在什麼地方，他們總是三句不離本行。

➲ Sandy yelled at her new husband for talking shop at their wedding.
珊蒂對著她的新婚夫婿大吼，因為他在婚禮上還不忘公事。

實用會話

A So, I think we will need to increase our sales territory. Otherwise, we'll never reach our third quarter goals.
因此，我認為我們必須擴展我們的銷售版圖。否則，我們永久也達不到預定目標的四分之三。

B Robert! Must you always talk shop? This is supposed to be a nice relaxing dinner with friends.
羅勃！你一定要不停地談公事才行嗎？現在應該是要和朋友們輕鬆用晚餐吧！

A I'm sorry, dear. You're right. I stand corrected.
我很抱歉，親愛的。妳說的對，我認錯。

B Apology accepted. Now tell the Smiths about our trip to France. What was the name of the town we went to?
我接受你的道歉。現在跟史密斯一家人說說我們的法國之旅，我們去的那個小鎮叫什麼名字？

t

* tattletale [n]

告密者

【負面】

中英文詳解

someone who always tells when someone does something wrong

當別人犯錯時，總愛告發別人過錯的人

➲ My sister is the biggest tattletale. She told my mom I broke the window.

我姊是個超級大嘴巴，她跟我媽說我打破了窗子。

➲ Don't be a tattletale and tell the boss that I wasn't really sick yesterday.

別去跟老闆告密，說我昨天不是真的生病。

實用會話

A I can't believe it. I was fired!

我實在無法相信，我竟然被開除了！

B What? Why?

什麼？怎麼會？

A I had been using the office computers to surf the internet after work and look for another job. They found out about it.

下班後，我用公司的電腦上網找工作，被他們發現了。

B How did they find out? Was there a tattletale?
他們怎麼發現的？有人告密嗎？

A Yeah, my coworker. He saw me last night and told my boss.
對，是我同事。他昨晚看到就跟老闆告狀了。

* teacher's pet

老師的愛徒

中英文詳解

to be the teacher's favorite; to be treated better than the other students
老師偏愛的學生；比其他學生受到更好的對待

➲ Tom thinks he's the teacher's pet and can't get in trouble for anything.
湯姆自認為是老師的愛徒，不可能遇到麻煩。

➲ Everyone tries to be nice to Sheila. She's the teacher's pet.
大家都試著親近希拉，因為她是老師的愛徒。

實用會話

A The teacher said I don't have to take the next exam, since I scored a 99 on the last one.
老師說我下次不必參加考試，因為我上次的考試拿到99分。

B That's because you're the teacher's pet.
那是因為你是老師的愛徒呀。

A What? No, I'm not!
什麼？不，我不是！

B Yes, you are. I scored 99 on that exam, too. She's still making me take the next one.
是啦，你是。我也考了 99 分，她還是要我參加下次考試。

MP3-34

* thick-skinned

[opp: thin-skinned]

厚臉皮的，神經大條的

【反義：thin-skinned】

中英文詳解

not to be easily upset or offended
不容易感到不開心或被冒犯

T

➲ You can say almost anything to Cindy and she won't get upset. She is extremely thick-skinned.
你可以對辛蒂口無遮攔，她不會不開心。她的神經異常地大條。

➲ I wish I was more thick-skinned. I always take things too personally.
我寧願我的神經大條一點，我總是把事情往自己的身上攬。

實用會話

A I can't believe you are not upset by what Joe said!
不敢相信你竟沒有因為喬所說的話而感到沮喪！

B Why should I be?
不然我應該怎樣？

A Because he insulted you and your family!
因為他羞辱了你和你的家人啊！

B His opinion is not important. Besides, he was upset.
他的看法不重要，而且，他很沮喪呀。

A Boy, you sure are thick-skinned.
真是的，你的神經太大條啦。

t

* time flies

時光飛逝

中英文詳解

time seems to move very quickly

感覺時間過得很快

➲ You know what they say, "Time flies when you are having fun!"

你知道大家說的：「快樂的時光總是過得特別快！」

➲ Is it 11 p.m. already? Wow, time flies!

已經晚上十一點啦？哇，時光飛逝啊！

實用會話

A Honey, what time is it?

親愛的，現在幾點了？

B It is only 10 minutes since the last time you asked me that question.

距離你上次問我，不過才過了十分鐘而已。

A Really? Wow! Usually time flies while I'm writing. I'm not sure why it seems to be going so slow right now.

真的？哇！當我在寫作時總覺得光陰似箭，不知道為什麼現在卻過得這麼慢。

B Maybe you need to take a break. Go do something fun and relaxing. Then you can start fresh when you get back.
也許你該休息一下，找些樂子，放鬆一下，然後再帶著飽滿的精神回工作崗位。

* tongue-in-cheek

毫無誠意；不認真

中英文詳解

insincere; joking
沒誠意的；開玩笑

➲ You can't ever take what Jonah says seriously. He is always making tongue-in-cheek remarks.
約拿說的話你可別太認真。他向來都沒當真。

➲ Please don't get upset. My last comment was tongue-in-cheek.
請不要生氣。我最後說的那句話只是玩笑話。

實用會話

A Did I just hear your son say that you were crazy?
我剛聽妳兒子說妳快抓狂啦？

B Yeah. It's not the first time he's said that to me.
對啊，那可不是他第一次這麼說我了。

A And, you aren't mad at him?
那，妳現在不生他的氣了？

B Why should I be? I know he loves me and it was just a tongue-in-cheek remark. We are always poking fun at each other.
為什麼我要生他的氣？我知道他很愛我，他剛剛只是隨便說說的。我們常常互相開玩笑。

A Ok, if you say so. But, I think I'd be upset.
好吧，如果你要這麼說。可是，我想我一定會生氣。

* two-faced [n]

表裡不一

【負面】

中英文詳解

to do or say one thing one time and something different another time

在某個時間做或說一件事，在另一個時間又做或說另一回事

T

➲ Richard is so two-faced. He has promised me many times to repay me the money he borrowed. But, he never has.

理查真是表裡不一。他已經答應我很多次要還我錢，可是他從沒做到。

➲ Mary acts like a nice person in front of her mother. But, she is really very naughty. She is so two-faced.

瑪麗在她媽媽面前表現得就像個好孩子。但是她真的非常頑皮。她實在是個雙面人。

實用會話

A I hate Anne. She doesn't know how to do her job, blames other people for her mistakes, and is always late for work.

我討厭安。她不知道怎麼做事，還因為她自己的不對責怪別人，又常常遲到。

B Yeah, I know. The only reason they hired her is she is the manager's sister. She is such a....

對啊，我也知道。公司會雇用她只是因為她是經理的妹妹。她真是個……

A Anne! How are you? Hey, great job on the Bremmer account. See you later...

安！妳好嗎？嘿，布梅爾那個案子做得真好。一會兒見……

B Wow. That was so two-faced!
哇，你真是雙面人耶！

MP3-35

U * underdog

處於劣勢的一方

中英文詳解

the person or team not expected to win or be successful
沒料到會獲勝或不被看好的人或隊伍

➲ The Miami Heat was considered the underdog. But, they actually made it to the finals.
邁阿密熱火隊不被看好，但他們最後卻打進決賽。

➲ The current president was the underdog in the recent elections.
現任總統在最近的選舉中曾是居下風者。

實用會話

A So, who do you want to win in the race today?
嗯，你希望今天的比賽誰獲勝？

B I'm cheering for the guy from Malaysia.
我要為馬來西亞來的那個男生加油。

A Really? He's not very good. I don't think anyone expects him to win.
真的？他的表現不是很好耶。我想沒有人認為他會贏。

B I know. But, I like cheering for the underdog. Sometimes they surprise you and win.
我知道。但是，我喜歡為表現處下風的人加油。有時候，他們會出乎你意料而得勝。

MP3-36

very thing

這件事

中英文詳解

the exact thing
就是這件事

➲ Julie got me the very thing I wanted for my birthday.
茱莉買了一個我很想要的東西當我的生日禮物。

➲ That cup of coffee was the very thing I needed to make it through this meeting.
那杯咖啡正是我需要的，好讓我可以撐過這個會議。

V

實用會話

A The boss drives me crazy sometime.
我的老闆有時簡直快讓我抓狂。

B Why? What happened?
為什麼？怎麼回事？

A In the sales meeting, he said that we needed to reorganize the department in order to improve our sales figures.
在業務會議上，他說，為了改善業績，必須重新整頓部門。

B So, what is wrong with that? It sounds like a good idea.
那，有什麼不對嗎？聽起來是個不錯的想法呀。

A But, it was my idea. I said that very thing 10 minutes before.
但那是我的意見。我在會議前十分鐘才提了這件事。

MP3-37

* well-off

[also: well-to-do]

手頭寬裕

【也做：well-to-do】

中英文詳解

wealthy; having a sufficient amount of money

富裕的；擁有充足的財源

➲ My boyfriend's parents are very well-off.
我男朋友的父母非常有錢。

➲ I don't need to be extremely rich. I just want to be well-off, so I don't have to worry about money.
我不想要非常有錢。我只要手頭寬裕，不用為錢煩惱。

實用會話

A Hey, congratulations! I hear you won the lottery.
嘿，恭喜！我聽說你中了樂透。

B Yeah. It was a complete surprise. I really didn't expect it.
是啊。真是令人意外。我可完全都沒料到。

A So, you are really rich now, huh? What are you going to do with all that money?
那，你現在可真是有錢了啊！你打算怎麼用這筆錢？

B Oh... I'm not rich. But, I am well-off. I shouldn't have to worry about money for the rest of my life.
噢……我不是很錢啦。只是，我變得手頭比較寬裕罷了。我這輩子不需要再為金錢傷腦筋了。

* wet blanket [n]

掃興的人或物

【負面】

someone or something that spoils other people's enjoyment
破壞他人興致的人或事物

➲ Please don't invite Tim to the party. He's is always such a wet blanket.
請不要邀提姆參加聚會。他總是很掃興。

➲ The news that we had to work on New Year's Day was a wet blanket to our holiday party.
元旦那天還要去上班的消息，對我們的假日派對來說，實在是很掃興。

實用會話

A Merry Christmas, Slater! Are you enjoying the party?
史拉特，聖誕快樂！你還喜歡這個派對吧？

B Uh... Merry Christmas, Zach. Yeah... I guess it is ok.
喔…聖誕快樂，薩克。是啊……我覺得還可以啦。

A What's wrong?
怎麼了嗎？

B Oh... it is just that the holiday is almost over and I have to go back to work soon.
哦……只是假期差不多結束，很快我又要回去工作了。

B Oh, don't be such a wet blanket. Enjoy it while you can.
喔，不要那麼掃興嘛。要懂得及時行樂。

* Wat's up?

近來可好？

中英文詳解

to ask what is going on, either as a general greeting or in concern
詢問近況，可以是一般性問候或關心致意

➲ Hey, Linda. I haven't seen you for weeks. What's up?
嘿，琳達，我好幾個星期都沒看到妳了。最近好嗎？

➲ Jerry, you looked depressed. What's up?
傑瑞，你看起來好沮喪。怎麼了？

實用會話

A Hey, Merlin. What's up?
嘿，瑪琳，最近好嗎？

B Ah... nothing much... I guess.
啊……還好啦……我想。

A Whoa! You don't sound happy. What's up? Why are you so sad?
哇！你聽起來不怎麼開心哦。怎麼了？你為什麼這麼難過？

B I'm sorry. I just broke up with my boyfriend.
對不起。我剛跟我男朋友分手了。

A I'm sorry to hear that.
真遺憾聽到這種事。

* wild-goose chase

徒勞無功

中英文詳解

a worthless hunt or chase

沒有意義的探索或追求

➲ We sent Joanne on a wild-goose chase to get her out of the office. She was starting to annoy all of us.

我們把瓊安帶出辦公室的心意，真是白費力氣。她開始煩我們每一個人。

➲ Trying to find the perfect gift for my mother has just been a wild-goose chase. She already has everything.

想找到一份很棒的禮物給我媽媽，真是白費力氣。她什麼都不缺。

實用會話

A How are the preparations for your trip going?

你的旅行準備得怎麼樣？

B Okay, I guess. But, I feel like I'm on a wild-goose chase.

還好啦，我想。可是，我覺得我可能是白忙一場。

A Why?
為什麼？

B Well... to get a visa I have to complete all this paperwork. Each piece needs to be signed by a different person, in a different office, in a different part of town. It is frustrating!
嗯……我要把這些表格文件都完成才能拿到簽證。可是每一份文件都需要由不同地方、不同辦公地點、不一樣的人簽名。實在很累人呀！

MP3-38

* window-shopping

〈只看不買〉逛街

中英文詳解

the habit of looking at goods in a store, often through the front window, without actually buying anything
習慣經常透過櫥窗瀏覽店裡的商品，卻不買任何東西

➲ Sometimes I just like to window-shop and see what's new in the stores.
有時候我只想逛逛街，看看商店裡有什麼新貨色。

➲ The mall wasn't open yet, so we just spent our time window-shopping.
商場還沒開，所以我們就先逛逛。

實用會話

A What do you want to do?
你想做什麼？

B Let's go shopping!
我們去逛街！

A Well... I don't know. I don't really have any money to spend.
嗯……我不曉得耶。我實在沒有錢花了。

B That's ok. We can just go window-shopping.
沒關係。我們還是可以四處看看呀。

A Nah... I hate looking at things when I know I can't buy them. Let's go to the movies.
不要……我討厭明知道自己沒辦法買東西還要去逛。我們還是去看電影吧。

* wishful thinking

一廂情願的想法

中英文詳解

believing that something is true just because one wishes that it were true

一個人只因為自己希望某事成真，就深信某事是真實的

➲ Believing that "Mr. Right" will find you is wishful thinking.
相信「真命天子」會找到你只是一種憧憬。

➲ Maybe I will get an A on the final and pass the course. However, I’m sure that is just wishful thinking.
我也許期末考會得 A，那門課就及格了。但是，我相信那只是我一廂情願的想法。

實用會話

A May I get you something else to drink?
還需要我幫你再送什麼飲料來嗎？

B No, it's ok. My date is two hours late and hasn't called.
哦，不用了。我約的人已經遲到兩個鐘頭了，而且一通電話都沒有。

A Perhaps he will still come?
也許他還是會來？

B That's what I've been telling myself. But, it is only wishful thinking. I've been stood up. Just give me the check, please.
我也是一直這麼告訴我自己。只是，那只是一廂情願的想法。我常常被放鴿子。請給我帳單吧。

A Very good, ma'am.
好的，小姐。

* with it [i]

時髦；反應快

【非正式】

中英文詳解

1. to be fashionable or up-to-date
2. to be able to think clearly or understand things (often neg.)

1. 時髦的或趕上潮流的
2. 能夠清楚地思考或了解事情（通常為負面之意）

➲ I don't think I like that shirt. It is not very with it.
我不喜歡那件襯衫。它不是很時髦。

➲ You have to say things slowly to John. He's not very with it.
你跟約翰講事情的時候速度要慢一點。他有點遲鈍。

實用會話

A How do you like my new sunglasses?
你喜歡我的新太陽鏡嗎？

B Ah... actually, I think they look kind of silly.
嗯……事實上，我覺得他們看起來有點呆耶。

A What? I think they are cool!
什麼？我覺得他們很酷耶！

B Oh, come on. Get with it! That style hasn't been in fashion for 20 years.
哦，拜託。跟上時代好不好！那個樣子已經褪流行二十年了。

A I don't care. I still like them.
我不在意，我還是喜歡。

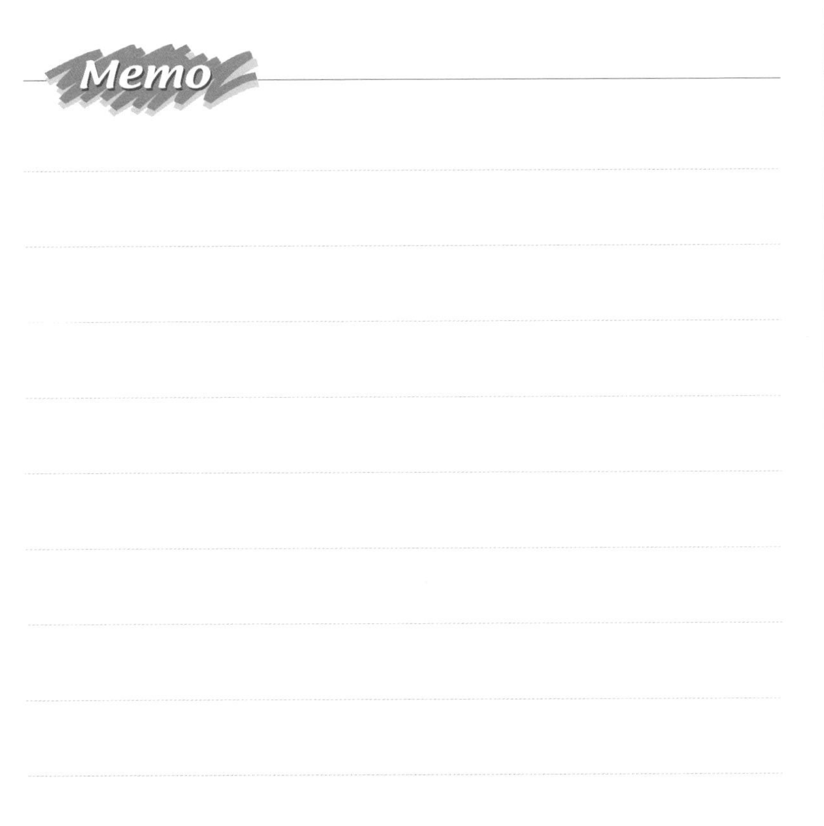

國家圖書館出版品預行編目資料

英文慣用語 / 喬納森 著. -- 新北市：哈福企業有限公司, 2024.06
面； 公分. -- (英語系列 ;90)
ISBN 978-626-7444-12-2 (平裝)
1.CST: 英語 2.CST: 慣用語 3.CST: 會話
805.18

免費下載QR Code音檔
行動學習，即刷即聽

英文慣用語
(QR Code 版)

作者／ 喬納森
責任編輯／張清芳
封面設計／李秀英
內文排版／林樂娟
出版者／哈福企業有限公司
地址／新北市淡水區民族路 110 巷 38 弄 7 號
電話／ (02) 2808-4587 傳真／ (02) 2808-6545
郵政劃撥／ 31598840
戶名／哈福企業有限公司
出版日期／ 2024 年 6 月
台幣定價／ 349 元 (附線上 MP3)
港幣定價／ 116 元 (附線上 MP3)
封面內文圖 / 取材自 Shutterstock

全球華文國際市場總代理／采舍國際有限公司
地址／新北市中和區中山路 2 段 366 巷 10 號 3 樓
電話／ (02) 8245-8786 傳真／ (02) 8245-8718
網址／ www.silkbook.com 新絲路華文網

香港澳門總經銷／和平圖書有限公司
地址／香港柴灣嘉業街 12 號百樂門大廈 17 樓
電話／ (852) 2804-6687
傳真／ (852) 2804-6409

email ／ welike8686@Gmail.com
facebook ／ Haa-net 哈福網路商城

電子書格式：PDF

哈福

哈福